Bone Beads

Bone Beads

LYDIA MACCLAREN

*"For everything there is a season,
and a time for every matter under heaven"*

— Ecclesiastes 3:1

To my husband, my stalwart support

Soli Deo gloria.

The ebook version of this book is available **FOR FREE** with subscription to email newsletter at **lydiamacclaren.com**.

CHAPTER 1

Leiv

"Y ou won't survive in this tundra."

She handed down the words like a prophecy, and it felt wrong to doubt them, but Liev did. He could survive. He had been raised there, the same as her.

Leiv could survive the tundra. He didn't know if he could survive her, because whenever Eirlin turned her resentful gaze upon him, he began to believe her words.

He arrived in Kaighton the same day as her tribe. He had intended to arrive early and help prepare the longhouse, but the winter came in harsh and forced the Kani down early from the slopes of the Heisel.

Since their arrival, she had not stopped questioning his

presence there. The eight other tribes joined the Kani, and now the flat rocky plains surrounding the longhouse transformed into a rippling field of tents. There they would rest for three months, feasting and celebrating the year they had been given.

Leiv should have felt jubilant to have finally returned after ten years, but her words haunted him. It wasn't just her he would have to survive, it would be all of the tribesmen who looked at him with vague confusion when he explained the census the capital had sent him there to conduct.

The census he had *convinced* the capital to conduct.

In the council room, standing before the elected officials, it had seemed straightforward. They needed a census. The southern lands knew all the data on the wheat they gathered, the sheep they slaughtered, and the grapes they picked; the nomadic tribes should know as well.

The tribesmen did not share his certainty, and collecting data was proving difficult when the nomads weren't used to tracking information. Armed with sheaves of paper, quills, and ink, he accumulated as much information as he could. But the more Leiv pushed for numbers, the more the older women began to spin rumors of his questionable mental state.

They might not understand the importance of the numbers, of the births and the deaths, the reindeer and the cloth, but he did. Those numbers could be the difference between life and death.

He was confident in his work, but sometimes it was easier to escape into the storeroom under the longhouse to count than endure the overly curious tribesmen.

"Have you supped?"

Leiv shifted uneasily on the stool, shuffling papers in his

leather-bound notebook, and pushed his glasses up his nose. The woman, Stalis, stood over him, eyes thickly rimmed with the creases of frequent laughter. Even now she had a quirked smile, as if her simple question held some secret jest.

"Not yet." He peered up at her, still attempting to discern what she asked without asking. "I wanted to finish tallying these up first."

"The salted fish?" A single eyebrow rose, solidifying that there was some joke.

"Yes," he responded stiffly, then felt a pang of guilt. She was a storyteller, as his mother had been, he should show her the respect of one. So, he softened his tone and attempted to explain. "No one can tell me what is in the storeroom. Someone needs to know."

"I suppose." Her response was kind. Whatever frustration had leaked into his words, it seemed to have gone unnoticed. "But they will still be here, while the food soon will not."

She motioned with her chin to the wooden ladder leading up to the main hall. Leiv glanced at his notes, then over to the dying flame of the oil lamp, then finally back to the patient woman. Her lips were still turned up in a smile; pleasant, but slightly distant.

They were all kind in that way. Four weeks he had been with them. He had been there to greet each tribe as they arrived with heavily laden sleds and a hungry host of reindeer. He had tried to be friendly, outgoing, and open, but they all looked at him as if he were some foreign oddity. Amusing, but in a fleeting way.

"I will come," Leiv said when Stalis' gaze remained firm.

"Wonderful!" Stalis snagged the lamp, and with a sharp snap of her layered skirts, she marched to the wooden ladder.

"Come along!"

From overhead, the tumult of voices filtered down into the storerooms, followed closely by the scent of roasted game. Leiv had forgotten to eat lunch, too distracted with counting, and the thought of meat stewed with carrots and potatoes made his stomach twist longingly.

With a sigh, Leiv consigned himself to an unfinished task and dinner spent crammed into a spot at the table. He wrapped the cord tightly around his journal and followed after the light.

His joints, stiff from too much sitting, groaned as he mounted the ladder. With each rung, the cool air of the cellar thickened with heat and laughter. Leiv emerged into the singular room of the longhouse. The long, low-roofed building was the only year-round structure in Kaighton, built to house one hundred people.

The tribe had grown to six thousand, and with so many, only the elders, storytellers, physicians, and their immediate families were invited each night to eat in the longhouse. Though overwhelming, it was good to see so many people crammed into the building. The population had nearly doubled in the ten years since the plague.

Large numbers did not protect against another plague.

Leiv forced the thought down with the barrels of salted fish, to be considered later, and instead focused on the uncomfortable task of finding a place to sit.

Twin fires roared in the two hearths on either end of the building, illuminating the heavily carved wooden beams crisscrossing over the heads of the throng. He couldn't count the number of people seated at the table running down the length of the room. Daughters sat on the laps of their fathers, mothers held infants, children wiggled between the legs of their parents, and older sons slipped back and forth to fetch soup for aging parents. The noise of the chatter roared around him, everyone in a match to be heard, making it even more difficult to think.

Stalis had replaced the lantern on its hook and had disappeared into the mess of bodies. She had a spot to return to, a family to welcome her back, and friends to sit beside.

He did not.

Leiv lowered the trapdoor and smoothed the woven rug over the top of it. He took his time. Though he hadn't checked, the room was so full he doubted there would be any room for him. He had only just glanced at the thick fur covering the doorway when a heavy hand clamped down upon his shoulder.

"Leiv!" a voice boomed, and he winced before he could school his expression. Quickly, he forced a smile and turned to face the elder with reddened cheeks, lively blue eyes, and a full black beard. The man beamed down upon him with his ever-present cheer, and Leiv stifled the guilt, knowing he had tried to avoid him.

"Eimon." Leiv returned the name as a greeting and faced the chief of the Kani tribe. Eimon was a kindly man, and since Leiv's arrival, the elder had taken great pains to ensure Leiv felt truly welcome.

There was nothing Eimon had done to make Leiv cringe at his presence, but his daughter was Leiv's ill-omened prophetess.

"Finished for the day?"

"About." Leiv shrugged, but the calloused hand didn't budge.

"Well, don't spoil your strength. Come!" The hand directed Leiv away from the door, down the table, and closer to one of the roaring fires. "Eat with us!"

Leiv's forced smile remained, even as faces turned upward to watch Eimon lead him closer. Remained even as his gaze bounced over each person, to the one he had hoped not to see.

Eirlin.

Her eyes were as blue as her father's, but they were cold as the winter ice. They flicked to her father, then back to him, and her expression hardened.

"Come," Eimon said again, and the others shifted to force room for the thick girth of their elder and the slim figure of the capital census taker.

"Fish didn't try to swim away?" Eirlin mumbled as Leiv sat across from her. Her eyes were so sharp, they cut, but she didn't break eye contact when she spoke.

"No," he said, but it sounded more like a question when it left his lips. A soft scoff, then she turned, and he was freed from her gaze.

Leiv sat beside an older man, a physician he believed was named Boden, and his middle son. The son's name would also start with a B, but he couldn't recall it. He did remember the two had an aptitude for wood carving and that the son had some beautiful wolves he carved from a fir tree.

"Boden," Leiv began, after accepting a bowl of soup from Eimon. "You are a woodworker, correct?"

"Correct." One of Boden's eyes was pale like the moon, and he had to turn to study Leiv with the clear one. "I'm surprised you recalled my name."

"I have a good memory." Leiv shrugged. Boden continued

to consider him, and now the son leaned around his father as well. "Though I must admit, I have forgotten your son's name."

"Brighton," the son offered, and Leiv slipped a hand from his warm bowl to tap it, open palm, against his chest. Brighton mirrored the action.

"You're both woodworkers, correct?"

"Correct." Boden took his good eye off Leiv and sipped his soup. "Just a hobby for long watches."

"Where do you get your wood?"

"Downed trees," Boden said; not harsh, but short.

"There are a lot of birches up in the northern woods," Brighton said, eager to discuss. "It's a great wood to work with, and our herds typically move up there during the summer."

"I see." Leiv smiled. The two men so embodied the Karish, they could have appeared in a university textbook on the tribes. "Have you ever considered selling your carvings?"

Boden and Brighton shared a glance.

"Why would a tribesman want it?" Brighton asked. "So many carve."

"Not here, down south," Leiv began, but then a smile curled on the old man's lips, and his excitement evaporated at the sight. "What?"

Boden chuckled. "They said you were excitable."

It was an uncomfortable statement because Leiv didn't know what it meant. It didn't sound like a compliment, nor did it have the sting of criticism. Leiv nudged his glasses up his nose and said nothing.

The man across from Boden tapped the table, calling for the physician's attention on a matter of ailing bulls. The conversation moved on, and Leiv was left with a head full of possible business ventures and unease over Boden's words.

Leiv stared down at his untouched soup, but the clawing hunger had vanished.

"Trying to change things?"

He looked back up at the question and found Eirlin's eyes filled with glacial hostility. To escape her question, he took a long gulp of the soup, mumbled his departure, and tore away from her glare and the crowded table.

A multitude of coats hung beside the door, and it took him too long to dig through and find his. It was dull compared to the bright red, green and blue hues of the others; colors easily seen against the snow. Such bright colors were unnecessary in a city, though Leiv hadn't noticed how the capital had shifted to more muted tones until he had first hung his coat in the longhouse.

Leiv felt even more set apart as he slipped on his dull blue coat.

Though he knew all the greetings, all the dances, all the lore, a barrier had been erected between him and his people. He had lived in the capital, or even further south, for the last ten years, but he was as much one of them as any of the other young men.

Still, he felt like a stranger.

It had snowed most of the day, and though there was a momentary pause, thick clouds still hung heavy over the earth. They blotted out any trace of stars and only allowed the faintest hue of moonlight to slip past.

A wide, well-tracked path led down from the longhouse and to the central bonfire. Leiv skirted the blaze, avoiding the tribesmen milling beside its warmth, and followed the path to where it split and branched into the camp. Each of the ten tribes had a separate campsite in a circle around the longhouse. His tribe, the Lantri, were situated to the northeast, and he veered his course to the side trail curling away into the night.

Eirlin's parting question looped in his mind, and he couldn't help but try to dissect the meaning she had laced into each word. But it wasn't her words that bothered him, it was her derisive consideration and the aloof smiles of the two men. He hadn't expected a grand welcome, but the expanse between his tribesmen and himself felt somehow more barren than he had expected. He was stranded on the tundra, and he didn't know why.

A single, fat flake of snow floated across his vision, and he paused amidst the silent row of tents and tilted his head up. More flakes descended after the first, thick and heavy.

He was alone in the storm.

CHAPTER 2

Eirlin

"I'm sorry for Ida's loss."

They were the first words she heard him speak, condolences offered to her father, and she bristled with each word. They were spoken with such familiarity, as if he understood anything, this census taker from the capital.

Then he turned to her, and she glowered at him, and she hadn't been able to stop. Even now, Eirlin scowled as Leiv pulled on his too-pale blue coat and left the longhouse. Anger warmed her chest and set her foot tapping against the furs spread over the floor. The hostility was unmerited. There was nothing Leiv had done *specifically*, but it felt good to have a conduit for her frustration, and he made it easy, so she glared at the flap, even after he was good and gone.

"You could kill with that look."

The cheery tone brought a bolt of guilt through her chest, and Eirlin tore her gaze away from the empty doorway. At her side, Neta sat, smiling; too large, too knowing.

"Come on." Neta laughed as Eirlin's glare morphed into annoyance, and she elbowed her gently in the ribs. "Were you listening to me at all?"

"Something about silk?" Eirlin asked, forcing her foot to still.

"Silk!" Neta repeated, clapping to emphasize the sheer wonder of the topic. "My mother took a few yards of it. If we start now, we could have dresses ready for the spring festival."

"Hmm," Eirlin mumbled because Neta expected mirrored awe. But Neta's words only turned her attention back to the census taker. He may not have deserved the hatred she heaped upon him, but he did epitomize all she loathed: the change the capital brought.

The silk was just another example.

"Fine." Neta rolled her eyes. "I'll get someone else to help me. You can't even finish Esala's belt, I doubt you'd be able to finish a dress even by this time next year."

"Hey!" Eirlin snapped and silenced her musings of the capital. "That's unfair."

Neta pursed her lips. "Is it untrue?"

"Of course," Eirlin muttered, but her friend just maintained a placid smile. Neta knew the truth, she always did. They had been raised alongside each other, and sometimes Eirlin suspected Neta understood her heart better than she did.

"How is Esala?" Neta asked; a question Eirlin knew would

come. One she had answered over, and over, and over again the last three weeks, usually with a noncommittal response.

"She's finally getting better," she truthfully told her friend.

"I knew she would," Neta said confidently. She slipped her hand into Eirlin's and gave a comforting squeeze.

Eirlin hadn't been as confident. Something deep inside of her was unsettled. Around her, the cheer was palpable, with the shrieks of delighted children and the laughter of old friends. But she was uneasy, and she couldn't pinpoint why.

Brighton said something to Neta, who chuckled and tossed a sarcastic comment back, but Eirlin wasn't listening. She looked down at her fingers interlaced with Neta's and wondered if her friend would be able to sort through her twist of emotions.

"Eirlin." Her father's call shifted her focus across the table. "Could you take this to your sister?"

In his hand was a bowl. She slipped her free hand from her own half-eaten bowl and took the soup.

"I need to help organize everything for the festival, now that all the elders are gathered. Otherwise I would take it myself," he continued, without looking at her.

"I understand." Eirlin smiled, though she knew it was an excuse. He had done all he could to avoid Esala, forcing her to bear the brunt of caring for the girl. She didn't fault him, she understood. She would stay away if she could.

The smell of sickness in the tent reminded them both of Ida.

Eimon offered a tight smile, then turned back to Veight at his side, ready to be distracted by organizing, planning, and preparing. Eirlin let a sigh slip through her lips, then squeezed Neta's hand.

"I'm taking this to Esala," she said as she rose. Her friend looked up at her with her too-knowing eyes.

"No." Eirlin's tone was sharp, and Neta's brows rose. She tried again, softer this time. "No, stay. Enjoy your meal."

Neta's eyes narrowed, and Eirlin left to retrieve her coat before her friend's perceptive gaze could find the root of anger growing in her heart. A few moments prior, she had wondered if Neta could untangle those same emotions, but now she turned away. She felt guilty, and she didn't want anyone to know how she feared for her sister and resented her in turn.

It was too ugly.

Instead, Eirlin escaped into the night, where the cold washed away emotions. In the deep winter chill, it was only possible to think about getting back to warmth. The night was thick and deep, and large flakes drifted down lazily.

Eirlin set out toward the eastern end of the camp, following the lamps swinging from the fibrous cords looped between the tents, lighting the way through the curve of the path as it spiraled through the camp. Each tribe circled their camp, warriors on the outside, the elder in the center.

It was a long, cold walk home.

High winter meant long nights and short days. The camp existed in a nearly endless night, lit by the stars above, when visible, and the lanterns below. It was a close, cramped place, always with someone tending to the herds or soothing a small child. Whenever Eirlin passed another, there was a smile and a few words as if between old friends, even if the passerby was a stranger.

Kaighton was more of a home, more of a community than she had for the other nine months of the year. Her spirits should have been high, but even the cold didn't seem capable of pushing aside the dark worries weighing down her soul. She saw fears in the fringes of the firelight, old tales of malevolent wandering spirits, and she could've sworn she heard the howl of a prowling wolf.

As she approached her family's tent, she took a deep, steadying breath. It was Esala's sickness making her uneasy. That was it. It must be. That was all. She repeated the assurances in her head because they didn't hold enough weight of truth to sink into her heart.

Eirlin yanked the flap of the tent back, sloshing soup over the edge of the bowl and onto her hand. She hissed in annoyance.

"Eirlin?" a brittle voice called from the darkness, nearly drowned amidst the shifting of furs.

"I'm here." Eirlin trained her voice to calm and slipped into the reindeer hide tent she shared with her father and sister. It was dark, the central fire pit only simmering embers, and she couldn't remember where she'd placed the lantern when she'd left Esala to rest. Thankfully, Esala did remember, and she lit the wick with a crack of flint.

Warm flame illuminated a hazy circle on Esala's face. Her eyes were bright, thick brows raised high as the young girl smiled up at Eirlin.

"Soup?"

"Soup," Eirlin said and sat beside Esala on the bed of furs. Hungry fingers snatched the bowl. As the girl slurped the soup, Eirlin slipped her fingers through her sister's dark tresses, straightening out the wayward curls and brushing the bangs back into place. "How're you feeling?"

Esala didn't immediately answer, too occupied with her

food.

"Good enough not to answer you, sister." Eirlin chuckled, and Esala grinned behind the bowl.

"I'm well," Esala said once the soup was finished. She looked down at the bowl longingly. "Well, enough to have gone to the table."

"None of that." Eirlin flicked Esala's nose, then stood and shed her heavy coat. "Don't blame father and me for wanting you to feel your best. Winter isn't the time for traipsing about sick."

"Yes ma'am," Esala muttered, voice heavy with frustration.

"I mean it." Eirlin unbuckled her belt and slid out of her fur vest. "It's cold out there."

She left her outerwear in a heap by the foot of the bed, though she knew her father would chide her. He liked order, Eirlin preferred comfort. She crawled beneath the covers beside her sister, pulling them all the way over her ear, so only her face was visible to Esala.

"You didn't tend the fire."

Eirlin stuck out her tongue and deemed Esala's frustrated comment unworthy of a response. Esala rolled her eyes but pressed no further. Instead, she set her empty bowl on top of the discarded clothes, sure to further irk their father, then pulled the blankets up around her as Eirlin had.

"I heard all the tribes are here now," Esala whispered. Eirlin closed her eyes and inhaled deeply the scent of fire, reindeer hide, and wild onion soup. "I'm glad to be well before the festival."

"As am I," Eirlin said, but it felt hollow. She was glad, but there was still a disquiet. It was because Esala was sick, she reminded herself. A lie.

"Is my belt almost done?"

"Almost," Eirlin murmured, though that was an exaggeration. "And the census taker is still here. You may still be able to meet him."

"Oh, good!" Esala leaped on the shift of topic. Eirlin hated bringing up the man, but she preferred to discuss him than the incomplete belt.

"He was counting the barrels of salted pike," Eirlin said. Esala had been enraptured by Leiv and his strange preoccupations, listening with glee as Eirlin recounted what new oddity he had performed. The younger girl didn't seem to notice the bitterness in her sister's voice.

"But why?" Esala giggled.

"Who knows?" Eirlin sighed. "But he's here to do it."

"Good, I want to meet him."

"Worry about meeting him later." Eirlin freed herself from the blanket cocoon to snuff out the recently lit lamp. "For now, let's rest."

Eirlin couldn't fathom what interest her sister had in the man. He may have been from the Karish, but he was a foreigner. His hair was cropped, just above his shoulders and tied back, unlike the long braids of the rest of the men, and his beard was trimmed close unlike the others. His clothes were crisp and streamlined, and his thick glasses perched ridiculously on the brim of his nose.

He belonged to the south, she had decided, and the south didn't belong in the north. This only worsened her frustration, because it was this foreigner who remembered her mother's name three years after her death.

She was glad he was leaving soon.

24

CHAPTER 3

Leiv

Leiv awoke to snow.

He opened his eyes and saw a drift of white sliding into the tent. Startled, he sat and squinted, until his wandering hand found his glasses. He slid them into place and confirmed snow was indeed invading.

A shiver slipped down his spine as the fur blankets fell about his waist. He heaved a sigh, lifted himself, shivering in the cold, and crossed the tent to the open flap. Last evening, he had left his boots at the entrance, and now they sat with snow on their toes.

Leiv shook off the boots, then slipped them on, cinching them tight around his calves, and began to kick as much of the snow out as he could.

"Morning!"

"You left the flap open." Leiv tried not to sound irritated, but even a young child quickly learned to secure the tent.

"I thought I'd be back sooner." At the contrite tone, Leiv relented, pausing in his kicking to look up at Falk.

He was everything a Karish man should be. Tall, broad-shouldered, with a plait down his back and a thick beard. Falk had kindly eyes, always had. They had known each other since childhood, raised in the same tribe. Falk's older brother, Forinth, had been Leiv's closest friend.

Leiv suspected Falk had offered for Leiv to stay with him out of a lingering sense of duty to his deceased brother. The same lingering sense prompted Leiv to accept.

"It's fine." Leiv waved aside the annoyance, not wanting to chastise the man in his own home. He was grateful for Falk's company when he wasn't off with his betrothed. "It's not that much snow."

"Not that much!" Falk barked a laugh. "Do you realize how much we got?"

Leiv shifted his gaze past Falk to the row of tents. Everything glittered in the early sunlight, sparkling white like the wall of glass tiles Leiv had once seen at university. He would have argued the scene in Kaighton was even more beautiful than the display of delicate glass, except the longer he looked, the more he realized just how much it had snowed.

It piled high along the sides of the tents, and tribesmen attempted to shovel out sloppy paths the wind quickly pushed back into the cleared space. Leiv glanced down to see that Falk wore snowshoes, even in the camp.

As if seeing all that Leiv calculated, Falk's smile fell.

"It's a lot, Leiv," he said. His breath bloomed white. There was too much whiteness; it clouded Leiv's thoughts.

"I have to leave this afternoon."

"Impossible." Falk shook his head, definitively. The word was too weighty for Leiv to connect with anything, and it was only after a few seconds of blank incomprehension that Falk added, "I'm sorry, Leiv. Kreilen was supposed to be back yesterday. There's just too much now. There's nothing we can do."

"Do," Leiv repeated, already running through alternate possibilities, anything to remedy the situation and present an agreeable alternative. He came up with nothing. "There's really too much snow?"

"Did you see those flakes last night?" Falk scoffed. "The last three days it's been like that. The roads are just too thick with it for a carriage of any kind to get through. You could probably do it yourself, but…"

Falk trailed off because they both knew it was impossible. Leiv had endured the most ribbing for the extent of his trappings. He had brought a carriage filled with gifts for the tribes; new inventions, supplies of paper and exotic cloth, all from the capital. Most remained untouched. Only the women took the cloth, not wanting anything to go to waste, but he had overheard them whispering about its durability, and clucking their tongues at poor insulation.

He'd just wanted the trip to go perfectly.

The present situation was less than perfect.

Stuck, for at least a week. Even as he reassessed his plans, he winced. It wouldn't just be another week. In another week, there would be more snow, which would make two weeks, and if there was even more snow, he could easily be trapped for a month. Or all winter, before the spring thaw began.

"I have to leave," he said, though it hadn't been intentional, simply a gut reaction as the various scenarios played out in his mind. They all ended with a missed deadline. A long-missed deadline. Worst case, missed by five weeks.

Very far from perfect.

"You can try to talk with an elder, but I don't—" Before Falk finished his thought, Leiv pushed past him and plunged into the calf-deep snow of the path, latching onto the singular title, 'elder.'

Leiv set his course for the longhouse, but with each step he sunk deep, too deep, a constant reminder that this was useless. Even an elder wouldn't be able to help.

But he had to try.

Around him, the camp roused. In winter, there were only five hours of daylight, and none were wasted. All tasks too difficult to perform in the light of a lamp were crammed into those short hours. Women sewed and embroidered, men stitched leather saddles and harnesses, and even the children were put to work sorting through whatever they had foraged from the nearby woods. No one was still.

Except for Leiv, who had no place in the camp, no household to care for, and no tribe duties to attend to, and already made up numbers to count as an excuse to stay.

Leiv caught sight of Eimon's stocky form in the corner of his eye, and he veered swiftly toward him. The elder walked down the path from the longhouse, toward his tribe's campsite. At his side was his older daughter, but even she didn't stop Leiv from calling out, "Elder Eimon!"

The elder turned and paused when he saw Leiv struggling to meet him. Eirlin turned a moment later, ice-blue eyes cutting with the full fury of the north wind. Leiv swallowed back the intimidation and forced out the words he had compiled for whichever elder he first met.

"I have deadlines in the capital I must meet, but I know the snow is quite deep. Is there any way…"

Eimon didn't have to say anything to silence him. Leiv saw the remorse in his eyes, the resigned attention he gave. He would have let the census taker finish expressing his concerns, but Leiv let the words die upon his tongue. His heartbeat was loud in his ears as Eimon's lips formed a thin, firm line, before parting to hand down a ruling Leiv did not want to hear.

"I'm sorry," he said, and Leiv believed him, though it helped nothing. "There is too much snow for Kreilen to return, or to get the wagon out. The only thing we can do is wait."

Leiv sucked in a deep breath of frosty air, then let it all out. He had nothing more to say. He regretted letting the wagon driver return when he asked for an extension of their stay. Regretted asking for the extension at all. He thought he had time, but he should have known.

"The capital should have known better," Eirlin mumbled, and he cringed at the berating words from another's lips. Eimon raised his brows and looked down at his daughter. She turned away from his stare but persisted nonetheless. "They should know how unpredictable the snow is."

"Hmm." Eimon sighed, but it was not quite an agreement. "Leiv, I am sorry. But until you can go, you are welcome here."

The elder set a heavy hand on Leiv's shoulder. It was supposed to be a gesture of comfort, but the shock of the weight rattled down to his bones, and he felt himself sink deeper into the snow.

"This is as much your home as it is mine."

Something else meant to comfort, but it only served as a reminder that he may belong, but there was no place for him.

"Come, Eirlin." Eimon lifted his hand from Leiv's shoulder and continued down the road. Eirlin hesitated a moment, gaze heavy upon Leiv, though he couldn't bring himself to meet it.

"You should not have come," she muttered, then trekked after her father. He sighed, shoulders falling, unable to muster the anger he should have felt.

It had been ten years since he had been in Kaighton, since he had been orphaned and sent to live with his uncle. He had hoped for a joyous reunion to the place, with his people, as he completed a task to protect them all.

Everything was going very much less than perfect.

CHAPTER 4

Eirlin

Eimon tried to use the distraction of the census taker to brush aside the topic, but Eirlin didn't let him. She trailed after her father, silently cursing his long legs and how quickly they crossed him over the high snow.

"You let her go back to her duties!" Eirlin snapped, bringing up the concern he hadn't yet addressed. He sighed, but she ignored it. "Her fever only broke two days ago!"

"She said she felt up to it," Eimon defended weakly.

"She's a child," Eirlin growled. She glared at her father's broad shoulders, angered he didn't even stop and look at her. "She doesn't understand that she needs rest."

"She's only a child for a few more weeks." The comment

only drew her ire, and she angrily chewed her lip. "Once past the ceremony, there will be more duties for her. She is eager, Eirlin. Let her be eager."

"I'd rather her be alive."

That did make her father stop. He turned to face her, and she regretted the comment. She pushed too far, she knew, but he had mentioned the coming-of-age ceremony, and the reminder that the deadline for the belt was so close only irritated her.

"I'm just concerned," she whispered. A rational part of her knew it was time for Esala to return to her duties, but the larger part, the part that felt the press of the unease, hated the decision. "I can manage her duties."

"No, you can't." Eimon's voice was gentle, which hurt more. She wished for his anger, to see her own frustration reflected in him. But he was always calm, which made him a wonderful elder. She was born like her mother. "You've barely managed it the last three weeks, and there are more preparations for the ceremonies. Now go, attend to your duties. I have made my decision."

His hand rested briefly on her shoulder, and she pictured the same placating gesture given to the census taker. She scowled at the thought and waited until Eimon was well down the path before moving to obey her father's orders. She didn't want him to see her dark expression.

She stewed in her anger, roughly going through the motions of her duties. While there was sunlight, she should sew more beads onto Esala's belt, but the thought of the meticulous work only filled her with more irritation, so she opted instead to fill the sled with hay for the reindeer.

Spite gave her strength, and she threw a square bale with

too much force. It thumped onto the wooden slats in a puff of dust. Eirlin winced, guilt welling and cooling the anger, just a little. She was being irrational, she knew, but it was hard to stop when she didn't know what else to do with the emotions.

"Woah," Neta mumbled, and Eirlin's shoulders slumped in defeat. She'd been blind to her friend's approach. "What fox carried off your dinner?"

"It's nothing." Eirlin tried to brush aside the question but knew Neta's eyebrows were raised even before she turned to face her. Not only were they raised, but her arms were crossed, and her head tilted as she patiently awaited the explanation she wordlessly demanded.

"Is it about the training offer?" she asked, and Eirlin cringed. The offer to join the training candidates should have been at the forefront of her mind. After all, such an offer was an honor, a chance to be trained and potentially earn a title as an elder, storyteller, or physician. She still hadn't responded to the offer, and she felt shame that the decision was the furthest thing from her mind.

"As much time as you need," Neta assured.

"I barely know," said Eirlin, relinquishing a morsel of truth. She rolled her eyes up to the heavy gray clouds promising more snow, and soon. "It's not the time to discuss, we're wasting daylight."

"I said as much time as you need."

"Later, I promise."

The brow inched higher, seeing the potential for an escape route, but Eirlin just shrugged, and Neta sighed. "Alright, but we *will* talk about it."

"We will."

Neta lifted the next bale, though she didn't need to help. In silence, they worked. Unspoken words burned on Eirlin's tongue, threatening to consume her, and she wanted to confess the whole truth to Neta, but she hesitated.

She wanted to wallow in the feelings, though she knew it was wrong, though she knew it was unhelpful.

"Thank you." Eirlin broke the silence when Neta set down the last bale. She pulled the sled away, and Neta let her go without pressing further. Eirlin had promised, after all, and Neta knew as well as she did that she could only avoid it for so long.

The sled glided smoothly over the snow, now compacted with the ruts of previous sleds as they hauled feed out to the penned reindeer. Eirlin followed the tracks, head down, simply focusing on the snow beneath her feet until she could make out the individual edges of each unique flake.

She focused on them, instead of the twisting in her gut, the uncertainty clenching around her chest, the unease gnawing at her soul.

The tracks led to the edge of the camp, where the most vulnerable of the Karish reindeer were housed in a fenced corral. Any reindeer sick or injured were held there to recuperate while the rest foraged in the forest. Most of the herds would descend further south, nearly to the capital. A few tribesmen from each tribe would follow after the herds, while the rest enjoyed the company of the whole community.

Eimon held a few deer in the corrals, marked on their ears with the unique cut of their family, so Eirlin stomped through the snow to assist in their care. When the wooden stakes of the fence burst through the snowbank, she tore her gaze from the ground.

And saw Leiv.

He stood beside the fence, finger jabbing at the air as he counted something she couldn't see, mouth moving in silent numbers. In his hand were papers. Always papers, always numbers, always counting, always assessing, always reporting back to that faraway capital.

What he counted now, after so recently learning he was stranded in the camp, she could not guess. Eirlin wondered what his judgment would be when all his numbers were sorted, and her life was weighed in the balance.

A shout broke her from the seething anger. Leiv jolted, turning but too late to avoid a collision with the dog barreling down the track. It yelped and Leiv stumbled, feet punching into a snowdrift, glasses slipping from the brim of his nose.

Eirlin heard it, the distinct crack of glass beneath the retreating dog's paw. Leiv's whole body stiffened. Everyone was still, no one daring to breathe as they waited for the reaction of the census taker.

When Leiv finally did move, his motions were slow and precise, carefully plucking the twisted metal from the snow. A boy, holding the dog firmly by its collar, shifted hesitantly closer.

"I'm sorry," he mumbled, cheeks red with embarrassment. "For breaking them."

"It was an accident," Leiv said. He kneeled in the snow, plucking each shard of glass and dropping them into his cupped palm. "It's alright."

"Can I…" The boy hesitated, uncertain of what to offer when no one knew the worth of the glasses.

"No, it's fine."

The boy retreated, head low with shame, dog wiggling for freedom. The other spectators snuck furtive glances and muttered gentle chastisements of the boy between themselves. Eirlin tugged her sled forward and stopped beside Leiv.

"What are you going to do now?" she asked as he stared down at his palm. "It won't be so obvious you're from the south."

Even she flinched at her jest, the words crueler than she intended. The ugly emotions inside her were satiated, but she pushed too far.

Leiv, however, didn't seem to have heard. He stood, gaze still transfixed by the broken glasses, face blank.

"Is it that bad?" Eirlin tried to soften her voice, to make up for the cruel joke. She failed. He glanced at her then, eyes narrowed just slightly, then looked back to his hand.

"Yes," he said simply. "I… I really can't see well without them."

"Hmm." Eirlin mimicked her father's frequent reassurance and hoped it had the same calming effect as when her father used it. "Well, what are you going to do now?"

"I…" His eyes bounced aimlessly around them but landed on nothing. "I don't know."

"I have a job for you," Eirlin offered, then regretted saying anything. It was hard to discern her motivations. It *was* a job, one he could do, whether or not he could see well. It was also a job she didn't want Esala to do.

His gaze landed on her, brow knitted together in distrust, and she couldn't blame him. Especially not when she waved her hand, dismissed her misgivings, and said, "Follow me."

CHAPTER 5

Leiv

"Don't worry, they're all weaned." Eirlin clapped a hand on his shoulder, then turned on her heel, and left him with the squealing children.

"Wait—" He twisted to catch her, but all he saw were dark shapes in his vision. He couldn't possibly identify which of the moving blobs was the elder's daughter.

There was an unnerving silence behind him, and he spun around to upturned faces. His eyes bounced over each blurred face, trying to assess the best course of action. Three boys and four girls, all around the age of three.

Infants were kept with their mothers, wrapped tightly to their chests as they worked. As the children became more wriggly, they were given to the older children to play with. When a child reached maturity at age thirteen, they would be given their beaded belt and expected to work alongside the adults.

Leiv was eleven years past thirteen. It had been so long since he'd cared for the younger tribesmen, and he could think of nothing else to do but stare down at their expectant faces.

"Who's in charge of you?" he asked, but the children just stared. Anxiety twisted his gut, and he was about to corral the whole lot of children to seek out Eirlin when he heard snow crunch behind him.

"Who are you?"

He whirled around to the young girl, half his size, with wild black hair trying to break free from her loose braid, and crystal blue eyes curiously considering him.

"Uh," he mumbled, unsettled by her familiar face, "my name is Leiv."

"The census taker!" She gasped. Everyone used the title in place of his name, though it made him uncomfortable. But she seemed so excited, he just nodded an affirmation.

"I've been wanting to meet you!" she continued as she slipped past him and into the shelter of the lean-to. The children scrambled to her, grabbing at the flatbread she brought for them.

"You have?"

"My name is Esala." She gently settled each child on the ground for their treat, brushing aside the commotion that overwhelmed him. "Elder Eimon's daughter."

"You look like your sister," he said, finally pinpointing why she looked so familiar. She had the same crystal eyes as Eirlin. But while the older sister's resembled cracking ice, the younger's were a calm lake.

Esala laughed as she sat beside the toddlers. "Thank you!"

Leiv shifted awkwardly, not sure why he had brought up the resemblance, and uncertain how to proceed. He still had to ask Esala about the job her sister put him to.

"It's nice to meet you." Levi finally settled on the greeting, backtracking to smooth over his odd comment. He tapped his palm against his chest, and Esala returned the gesture, then patted the carpet. He sat beside her and stiffened as a boy plopped into his lap.

"My sister says you're counting everything," Esala said.

"Not everything," Leiv muttered, feeling the need to defend himself against anything Eirlin would say of him.

The boy in his lap offered a half-eaten piece of bread, and Leiv politely shook his head. The boy didn't seem to understand, and pushed the seasoned bread against his lips. Leiv took the piece, and the boy contentedly slipped off his lap and toddled back to the wooden blocks scattered around the rug.

"It's fascinating," Esala said. "I've never heard of so much counting."

"It's helpful," he said, but there seemed to be genuine curiosity so he continued. "It's helpful to know what we use, what we need. If anything happens, we know what we need to survive."

"We've never done that before, and we're still here."

"That doesn't mean it wouldn't have helped us," he said, words slow. The question was common, but rarely did he hear this curious, open tone. She was young, but he had gone to the university at a young age too, only three years after his ceremony, two years after he had moved to the capital.

"The tribes initiated the capital for the very reason of strengthening our boundaries," he said. "A simple way to strengthen ourselves is by knowing our numbers and what we require. We would know what resources were needed if there was a famine, for example."

Or a plague, his mind offered, but he stifled the thought.

"You think it would help just knowing?" she asked, running her fingers through the tangles of toddler curls.

"I do," he whispered. Famine, drought, flood, plague—it was all possible, and all unpredictable. He would do anything to keep more children from becoming orphans. Esala nodded at the two grave words and seemed to understand the weight of his own contemplations.

"It's a wonder," she murmured. "All the things to consider."

"Exactly." Leiv nodded. "And if we want to protect ourselves, we have to consider it all."

Tiny antlers of a wooden reindeer scrapped against his cheek. He jerked back from the little boy's adamant hands, but the boy pushed the animal closer.

"He wants a story." Esala smiled. "He loves stories."

"Stories?" Leiv repeated, but it was hard to get the word past his lips when his mouth was so dry. He licked his lips as he looked down at the boy's wide, pleading gaze.

"You don't have to," Esala said. "I can."

"No," he said quickly, then offered a shy smile. "I would like to try."

There were many stories Leiv knew, many he could share. The little reindeer reminded him of a particular tale, one his mother had told him many times when he was the same age as the little boy. So, he took the wooden reindeer, then picked up a wolf lying nearby.

"I know a good one about a wolf and a reindeer," he began, then recited, "Late one winter night…"

It was how all their stories began, because it was how all the best stories began, though it pained him to hear the line in his voice instead of his mother's. As the words spilled from his lips, they painted a vibrant picture of the tundra and, at last, he felt at home.

CHAPTER 6

Eirlin

"Eirlin."

Her father's voice was gruff, and from the tone, she knew he had come to rebuke her. She glanced up from the thread, then back down. Her father's gaze was dark clouds promising a blizzard.

It had begun to snow. Heavy, thick snow. The day had prematurely darkened, and she scrambled to complete the section of the belt she had promised herself she would finish that day. Now, she sat too close to the lamp in their tent, with pricks in her fingers and a half-finished job.

Her father waited for her to respond. He stood at the entrance of the tent, arms folded and patiently waiting. He was such a patient man. With a sigh, she let the needle rest on the unfinished belt.

"Yes, father?"

"Why is Leiv caring for children?"

She smirked as she envisioned him, with his well-ordered clothes and neatly combed hair, amidst the chaos of small children. It would be a sight to behold.

Spite. The answer to her father's question was spite, but she couldn't say that. She picked up the belt and pulled the thread tight to secure the bead.

"Is caring for children below him?" she said instead, which wasn't much better.

"No." Eimon's voice was careful and calculated. "However, there are other tasks better suiting his unique skill set."

"What skill set?" She scoffed, then bit her cheek, closed her eyes, and waited for the admonishment she knew would come.

"Eirlin." Her name, spoken in a disappointed tone. "You are being childish."

She knew, but those nasty emotions inside of her roiled, and Leiv brought all the change she feared.

"Eirlin?" Her name again, but this time with a gentle nudge of a question. Asking to be let in, just like Neta, whom she had avoided. Eirlin sighed, set the belt beside the lamp, and lifted her gaze to meet his. His eyes were as rich as the earth, and just as steady.

"I know," she whispered. Her father sat at her side and waited as she took a moment to collect the tumult of thoughts. "I'm sorry."

"I'm not the one you should apologize to."

She looked away, into the shadowed corners of the tent. The thought of asking forgiveness from the census taker was a bitter one. To admit to him that she had been ugly made her cringe.

"What's on your heart, little songbird?"

The nickname brought hot pain to the back of her throat, and she swallowed against it. Her mother had given it to her, laughing that her first daughter had cried so much as a newborn she had to pretend it was the beautiful song of a bird.

"I don't like it," Eirlin confessed in a small whisper. "The change. It's all so much, and I'm afraid of what it will bring."

Eimon drew in a slow breath, ribs expanding and deflating, and he nodded. "I am too."

"Then why did the elders agree to establish the capital?"

"Because our world is changing." Eimon tipped his head down, considering his calloused hands. "We can't live in ignorance of that. We can't control the change, but we can control how we respond."

She knew. She had been there when the elders had announced the plans and when they had appointed the officials from their elders, physicians, and storytellers. The relief that flooded her when her father's name was not called to serve was still a palpable taste of fresh spring water on her tongue.

"I still don't like it."

She expected him to chide her, but at the admission, Eimon just sighed.

"I understand," he murmured, then lifted his head and looked at her. She straightened at his side, uncertain of what he evaluated in her. "How long have you had these thoughts?"

Eirlin didn't answer, unsure if she should answer from the decision, or from when the census taker arrived. Her father saw the hesitation and shook his head, looking back down at his hands.

"I didn't know your fears. I have not been there to support you," he murmured. "I am sorry."

"No, father, it's not—"

"No, Eirlin. I left you with the care of Esala and your duties, and didn't even realize you were struggling. I am sorry."

Eirlin chewed her lip, watching her father who still sat with his head bent.

"I forgive you," she whispered. She had been selfish, thinking only of her fears without even considering they may be shared by another. She had been selfish to think she was the only one struggling. So, she added, because she knew it would cheer him, "I will apologize to him."

A small smile quirked her father's lips.

"You are tenacious." He straightened and set a hand on her head like he did when she was a child. But instead of mussing her hair, he slipped his hand down to cup her cheek. "Use that tenacity to build us up."

With those words, he departed. The echo of his voice circled in her head. The anger, the resentment, the fear—it all felt insignificant when she considered the love in his voice, the encouragement he left her with.

She had been awful to the census taker. To Leiv.

Eirlin groaned and collapsed onto the bed. She had to apologize for the harsh barbs and glares. She threw an arm over her eyes and groaned again.

Build us up. It was a common refrain, an encouragement to care for the tribe. Her father had extended the invitation to join the candidates, and meanwhile, she had done the least candidate-like thing imaginable. She loved her tribe; loved it enough to admit that taking out her pain on one of its members was foolish.

Even if he did look like a southerner.

"Enough!" she growled and smacked her palm against her forehead. "Do better."

He was tenacious too, after all. She had never seen someone count as many things in such a short amount of time. It was a small concession, but she would give it to him because he was one of them.

Which meant she had to apologize.

48

CHAPTER 7

Leiv

"An interesting game."

Leiv startled at Eimon's voice and scrambled to sit, forgetting the three toddlers giggling on his back.

"Elder!" He tapped the little legs of the closet toddler. She squealed and scrambled away, the others scattering after her, and Leiv hurriedly stood. From the back corner, he heard Esala chuckle with the same cadence as her father. "I hadn't noticed you entered."

The darkness made the blurry world infinitely more difficult to understand. In the glow of the children's lean-to, Leiv could see well enough, but past the circle of their lamp light, everything was a dark smudge. Even now, the elder was a twist of pale skin and a bright red coat.

"I heard your glasses were broken," Eimon said, his deep, rumbling voice unmistakable. "I'm sorry to hear it."

"As am I." Leiv smoothed the wrinkles of his vest from the push and pull of little hands. His palm swept across something wet, and he suppressed a shudder. "I feel quite useless without them."

"I would say caring for children is rather useful, wouldn't you, Esala?"

"Absolutely!"

"I didn't mean…" Leiv fumbled and reached to push his glasses up the bridge of his nose, but found nothing.

"Don't worry, I understand." The elder chuckled and waved a hand in a blur of motion. "Come, I have a task more appropriate for your skills."

"Whatever would be of help," Leiv said evenly, though relief flooded him at a change in duty. His university math courses had not prepared him for the disorder of toddlers.

"Thanks for your help!" Esala chirped, and Leiv offered her a grateful smile. Though he was glad for a change of duty, he had genuinely appreciated her willingness to tolerate his bumbling efforts to help. Her features were a haze, but there was a smile on her face, that much he could see.

He left the comfortable warmth of the lean-to and followed the elder into the chill of the campsite. Though dark, it was not yet night, and activity swirled around him. The next evening was the festival, and the tribesmen rushed to finish the preparations. Leiv walked quickly through the commotion, not wanting to lose sight of the elder in the obscurity of his vision.

"I am thankful," Eimon said as he led Leiv through the tents of the Kani tribe. "It's admirable to be so willing to perform tasks meant for others."

"Oh." Leiv coughed, uncomfortable with the praise. "It wasn't… I just didn't know what else to do."

"You make that seem like a negative thing." Eimon halted and Leiv followed suit. When Eimon turned, he was close enough for Leiv to discern the smile crinkling the elder's eyes. "It's good to want to help."

"Of course." Leiv shrugged. "To build us up."

The smile blossomed into something more, but Eimon turned and swept aside the flap of a rectangular tent before Leiv could understand.

"Merkia!" Eimon called and ushered Leiv inside.

The tent was filled with chaos, more chaos than the children's lean-to. Long, rectangular tables filled the space, skewed at awkward angles, filled with an assortment of dried herbs and spices. Drying branches swung from ropes strung overhead, stirring as the chill breeze slipped in through the open entrance. The smell of the tent was pungent, a mixture of sweet, savory, and spicy.

Leiv's nose itched, and he wanted to step back and abandon whatever task Eimon had for him. He certainly didn't want to follow Eimon in deeper. His vision was murky, and he feared knocking into some oddly placed plant.

"I am here, Eimon," a brittle voice called from a far corner, feminine and elderly. Leiv squinted in her direction, but could only make out a vague outline of a small, hunched woman. "What have you brought me?"

Eyes fixed on him, and he balked. Though blurred, the woman's stare was unnervingly straightforward.

"This is Leiv," Eimon said.

"Ah," the woman crooned. "The census taker."

"A pleasure, grandma." Leiv lifted his hand to his chest.

"That title." Merkia waved a sprig in the air, crisp leaves rattling. "Am I so old? Come here, boy."

Leiv picked his way toward her, zig-zagging through the tables. When he reached her corner without incident, he lifted his gaze and was caught beneath her steely regard.

"Interesting."

Leiv blinked at the single comment.

"Hmm." Eimon hummed behind him as if he agreed. But with what, Leiv still didn't know.

"Why don't you grow a beard?" Merkia asked.

The directness of the question startled him, and his hand shot up to graze the closely-shaved stubble.

"I…" He glanced back at Eimon, but he just observed without any support. Leiv looked back down at the very serious countenance of the older woman. "I grew to like it this way during university."

"Interesting," she said again.

"I will leave you two." Eimon chuckled. "Leiv, assist physician Merkia with the herbs. She is very precise, I'm sure you will be of use to her."

He left Leiv with the stooped grandma who appraised him as if considering the worth of a young reindeer bull.

"How can I help you?" he asked.

"They say you don't have a wife," she said instead of answering. Heat blossomed in his cheeks, and he looked anywhere but her keen eyes.

"I do not."

"A betrothed, then?"

"No."

She *tsked* and turned back to the dried sage in her hand. She didn't say anything more and gave no directions, just gently plucked off each brittle leaf.

"I just completed university," he said, feeling the need to explain in the prolonged silence. Merkia gave no affirmation she had heard, so he continued. "I went to the south to study math. It's very rigorous, and… and this is my first time back in the north. Well, past the capital."

"And all you brought back with you was an odd beard fashion?" She lifted an eyebrow, unimpressed with his defense. The heat in his cheeks intensified.

"Here." She tossed him a small leather bag. "All these herbs need to be sorted and categorized. I'm sure your university education will suffice for that."

"It will," he mumbled and began to slip the sage leaves she had plucked inside.

"And as you can see," she continued, "we have a lot of work. Since you have no woman to tell me about, find another topic of interest."

"Oh." His voice trailed away, uncertain what may interest her.

"Tell me about the south," she prompted, and her words halted his hand.

"You… want to hear about it?"

"Why wouldn't I?"

"No one else seems very interested."

"Because," said a new voice, and at the sound of it, Leiv stiffened. His eyes sprang up from the leaves to the dark form at the entrance of the tent. "No one is interested in what the south is doing."

"Ah, Eirlin," Merkia said smoothly, as if the woman's words were not sharpened like blades. "Another with no interesting tale to tell. Did your father send you?"

"No," she said. Leiv steeled himself for another sarcastic remark prepared especially for him. But there was a pause, and instead, she continued. "I was simply passing by."

"And where are you headed?" Merkia asked.

"To help with the reindeer." Without the sting of ridicule, her tone was pleasant. His frown deepened at this conundrum, and he squinted to make out the wild curls eternally escaping from her braid. "Don't strain your eyes."

Those words, in a more familiar tone, were directed at him. He flushed and looked down, self-conscious of all his consideration of her.

"Can you tell your father to send Haila?" Merkia said, ignoring the last comment. "The herbs for the festival are ready."

"I will."

When he peeked back up, her dark shape had left. He blinked, certain he saw incorrectly, but she was truly gone. He wondered when she had arrived, and how much she had overheard of Merkia's personal questions. She needed no more kindle for her barbs.

"An odd one, much like you." Merkia chuckled. "Now, census taker, tell me a story."

CHAPTER 8

Eirlin

"Why don't we celebrate the gathering after the ceremony?" Esala grumbled. Her arms were heaped with the vibrant green elder shawl for her father, who had been too busy with preparations to come and retrieve the garment.

"Just makes the anticipation all the greater for next year." Neta tapped Esala's nose and winked. "Now get those to your father, he'll be needing them soon."

Esala's lips still turned down in a frown, but she obediently slinked from the tent with the armful of cloth. Once the younger girl had departed, a heavy atmosphere settled into the space. Eirlin sat cross-legged on the ground before the small mirror she had propped against the side of the tent and pretended she didn't notice.

Leaning close to her distorted reflection, she slipped a red dye across her lips until they were red like cranberries. The color was time-consuming to make, a mixture of beeswax and red leaves, and only used for this specific night. Red was said to be an alluring color, and all the marriageable women would paint their lips. While the great bonfire was officially a feast to celebrate another year of life, it was commonly recognized as a way to meet potential spouses from across the tribes.

Eirlin had not cared about the tradition since her mother had passed only three years past her coming-of-age ceremony. She cared even less when Neta's hard gaze bore into her back.

"So," her friend finally began, "are you finally going to explain? Or are you going to run away again?"

"No." Eirlin sighed and closed the small wooden jar of stain. She set it back beside the mirror, then shifted to face Neta. "I'll tell you."

"About time," she huffed, planting herself in front of Eirlin. From an inner pocket of her reindeer hide coat, she produced a jar of stain. "Please."

Eirlin took the proffered jar, thumb running over the familiar carvings. Neta had begun to prepare for the festival with Eirlin the year her mother passed. They never discussed why, but they both knew. Eirlin suspected that Neta's mother, already busy with four other daughters, didn't mind that her eldest went elsewhere to prepare.

When she looked up from the jar, Neta sat with an even gaze. Her hair was already braided, eyes already outlined with black coal, wolf pelt shawl already wrapped over her shoulders, all she needed was the red stain. She waited patiently. Simply waited.

"I am nervous," Eirlin admitted. She took the lid from the jar and dipped her pointer finger into the stain. "I feel like our life is changing, and I'm very much out of control."

Pushing back the emotions welling in her throat, she focused on slipping the stain over Neta's lower lip. It was good to have something to do, to distract her. She suspected that was why Neta had given her the task.

"I have only seen how things have changed," she continued when the pain had abated enough to speak. "It makes me fearful."

"I'm sorry, Eirlin," Neta murmured when Eilrin pulled her finger away for more stain. "And Leiv?"

Eirlin cringed at the name. Of course her perceptive friend would have noticed the ill-mannered interactions. She chewed her lip as she applied more stain.

"He just… was all the change I feared." She shrugged, wishing she could better explain. It was difficult to speak of the anger, hatred, and rage that had twisted her. It was her fault, and she had to face the consequences of her childish actions. "I was rude to him because it made me feel like I could do something about my fear."

"But?" Neta pressed. Eirlin set the lid back onto the jar and grabbed the mirror, presenting it to Neta. She inspected her reflection only briefly, before glancing back to Eirlin, refusing to relinquish her heavy consideration.

"But I was wrong." Each word was forced through her constricted throat. She had already admitted to her father, but each word still felt shameful. She couldn't imagine apologizing to Leiv himself. "He is one of us, and I was being cruel for things he has no control over."

"I do understand," Neta confessed, laying the mirror on her lap. "With all the changes the capital is making, it's easy to think everything will just… slowly crumble."

Heat pounded through her, and for a moment, Eirlin's vision went watery; Neta's words fanning the embers of fear.

"But," Neta continued, and her pale gray eyes lifted to meet Eirlin's, "we are a strong people. The creation of the capital is a testimony of that. We will not be destroyed, we will adapt, and we will be stronger for it."

Eirlin smiled, a shaky uncertain thing, and Neta met it with her own confident one.

"Thank you," she whispered, and Neta's fingers curled into her own, squeezing tightly.

"And Leiv?" Neta repeated her previous prodding, and Eirlin groaned.

"I have to apologize."

"That's simple enough." Neta's hand slipped from Eirlin's, and she set the mirror back against the tent. "Just say sorry."

"It's not that simple." Eirlin sighed.

"It could be." Neta winked and stood, brushing her coat smooth. "Ask him about triangles, he loves those."

"How do you know that?" Eirlin frowned.

Neta laughed and shook her head, then grabbed Eirlin's arm and hauled her up.

"Just because you were so set on hating him, doesn't mean I couldn't be pleasant." Neta smoothed Eirlin's coat, adjusted her belt, then nodded as if something had been decided. "Now come, we have a bonfire to enjoy!"

Eirlin let Neta's cheer pull her from the tent and down the aisle of the camp. There was a thrum in the air, a spark of life, though the night was deep and the cold heavy. A glow emanated from the longhouse, a brighter spot of orange beaconing to the tribesmen. Young children still darted between the tent stakes, but soon their mothers would call them to bed, and they would sleep, and only the belted tribesmen would feast, drink, and celebrate another cycle around the sun.

The two friends turned a corner, and Eirlin could see the blaze before the longhouse. Even from halfway down the aisle, she could feel the heat radiating from the crackling flames. Light flickered off the intricate carvings of the wooden doors of the longhouse. They were only shut at night, during the day the reindeer hide stretched across the entrance to allow easy access. But tonight, when the festival began, the doors would be thrust wide to welcome all inside to cycle between feasting and dancing.

Men still piled wood onto the blaze and women bustled to and from the longhouse, while the elders rolled out barrels of mead. Soon the festivities would begin.

As Eirlin and Neta passed the last of the tents, Eirlin caught sight of a tangle of black curls. She tugged Neta to a halt, then pointed toward her sister slinking along the edge of the clearing. Neta followed her finger, then nodded.

"Go talk with her, I'll find you later."

Neta continued toward the bonfire, while Eirlin veered her course to intercept Esala. As she approached, Esala noticed her and paused with a smile. Her arms were empty, and she looked taller without the large shawl.

"I won't be back too late," Eirlin promised and planted a kiss on her sister's forehead. The girl shrugged away from her sister's affection with a wry smile.

"Don't worry about me," Esala said and shifted to move

past Eirlin.

Eirlin caught her shoulder and Esala paused, tilting her head in question. Eirlin cleared her throat and thought about how to compose her awkward question. She didn't want to ask Neta, who would turn that knowing smile upon her. *It could be simple.*

"Have you seen Leiv?"

Esala's eyebrows scrunched in confusion. The exact reason she had avoided Neta's help. She wanted as little stir over this needed apology as possible.

"Umm…" Esala's eyes swept over the clearing, but she shook her head. "I haven't."

"That's fine." Eirlin released her hold on Esala's shoulder and tried to cover the disappointment with indifference.

"Why do you want to find him?"

"Something I need to say." She sniffed, but the guilt pressed against her heart. The half-truth saved face, but it was she who had done wrong. So, she sighed, and said, "I need to apologize, for being… harsh."

Esala smiled and Eirlin turned away to face the bonfire.

"You'll find him," Esala said. "And you know… I think you would even like him."

Eirlin snapped a sharp glare at Esala, but she just kept smiling. "Why?"

"Why not?"

"Don't you find him…" Then Eirlin struggled for the right word. One that was true and not twisted by her fears. "Odd?"

"Maybe a little." She chuckled. "But he's kind, and a good storyteller."

"Storyteller?" Eirlin asked, not able to envision the grave

Leiv speaking about anything other than numbers. But Esala nodded earnestly and Eirlin sighed. If Esala had a positive view of Leiv, it was her fault. She had placed them together, after all.

There was nothing wrong with liking the man. It seemed she was the only one who didn't.

"Get to bed," Eirlin muttered and stalked away, not wanting to face Esala's mischievous smile.

"Let me know how things go!"

Eirlin cringed at the shouted words but refused to look back, refused to answer, refused to make the apology anything more than it was.

The bonfire flared higher. As the children succumbed to sleep, musicians stepped forward and began to test their willow flutes and tap their reindeer skin drums. With the first rustlings of a song, more tribesmen streamed into the opening, their chatter a lilting tune beneath the instruments.

With more people, it would be harder to find the census taker, so Eirlin quickened her pace and circled the opening, eyes roving over the faces cast part in the night and part in the firelight. She curved around the fire to pass before the still-closed doors, when she saw him, sitting on a bale of hay at the fringe of the bonfire glow, nose buried in his notebook.

Her stomach twisted at the sight of him, and she almost turned away instead of facing her own actions. She forced her failing feet forward. He didn't glance up as she approached.

She thought of how Leiv had stiffened when he heard her voice while helping grandma Merkia. It felt like a slap, to see someone grow so cold at the mere sound of her voice.

She had done that herself. She deserved it.

Eirlin was nearly upon him now, but still he didn't look up, engrossed in whatever was marked on his pages. Her mind turned over every apology she could think of, trying to find the words that sounded gentle, soft, and kind. Then she stood before him and found she had no idea what to say.

"Are you going to sit here all night?" she asked, then cursed herself. It was not soft, gentle, or kind. He frowned, and his eyes flicked up to her, only briefly, before he hunched his shoulders and focused back on the figures.

"Perhaps."

It was an icy word, but she schooled her frustration. She merited his anger. She *had* called him a southerner.

Build us up.

"What are you doing?"

He paused, blinking rapidly as if he didn't know the answer to her question. He glanced up again, eyes narrowed, and she lifted her eyebrows and tried to express genuine interest. Perhaps not genuine interest in his notes, but at least genuine interest in mending their turbulent acquaintanceship.

"Making notes about the herbs Merkia is preparing," he finally said and swiped a thumb over his numbers. "It was interesting what she found important."

"Hmm," Eirlin said, to give her time to think of what to do with the statement. "That sounds like something to do when you're not at a festival."

He didn't reply. She sighed; she was not good at getting on his good side.

"Why aren't you dancing?" she asked. She could have just offered a clumsy apology, then departed to find Neta, but that felt as bad as what she had been doing. Words felt inadequate, but if she could prove she was sincere, perhaps he would accept her apology.

"I can't," he said, short and dismissive.

"Can't dance?" she asked, though she didn't believe it. All of their dances had steps, and anyone could learn them. To be a poor dancer would be a feat in itself.

"Can't see." He snapped the journal shut, and waved it toward the fire where couples had begun to dance. "I couldn't, even if I wanted to."

She had forgotten. Belatedly, she wondered if he was even able to see her from where she stood. With a swift step forward, she kneeled in front of him. He jerked back, eyes jumping over her face as he searched for her motives.

At least he could see her.

"Do you want to?" she asked. His lips parted, closed, then his eyes skipped to the bonfire behind her shoulder, before resting back on her.

He didn't respond, but she knew the look in his eyes was longing.

"Come on." She nudged his knee, and his eyes snapped to the point of contact. "Take my hand, I'll be your eyes."

He looked back up, mouth slightly agape. The moment stretched, and her empty palm tingled with the chill night air.

"Why are you doing this?" he finally asked, the question she had waited for. He studied her face, and she found she couldn't hold his intense gaze and looked down at her palm.

"As an apology," she murmured. "I know I've been… rather awful to you. I… I'm sorry."

Silence. Panicked curiosity forced her eyes up, needing to know how the awkward apology had been received.

Amber honey, the color of his eyes.

The recognition shocked her. For all she had constructed her opinions of him, she had never actually looked at him. He had simply been foreign. But there, with the firelight, the dark coal around his eyes, and the warm honey, she saw everything that made him part of her life.

The hay cracked as he set down his journal. He looked at his hand pressed against it for a moment. Slowly, he slipped his fingers off the leather.

Then he took her hand.

CHAPTER 9

Leiv

L eiv hadn't danced since the winter his parents died.

All the steps were seared into his mind, a piece of his childhood he could never forget. With each beat of the drum, the paces flitted into his mind, and he moved through them with a fluidity he had not expected.

He didn't know why he had taken Eirlin's hand. He tried to follow his reasoning; why she had offered, why he had accepted. But concentration was difficult when sleigh bells jangled in rhythm, when laughter cascaded around him, when a log cracked deep within the fire, when the tension of their interlocked hands pulled him back to her.

Home.

The feel of it settled within his chest. He felt at home, there in the throng of dancers with Eirlin's fingers tight around his. Around him, people moved in and out of clarity, but she was clear-cut at his side. A smile curled her lips, stained deep red, and more and more black curls escaped from the braid crowning her head.

Then she stood still, and he nearly collided with her. Her ice-blue eyes captured him, and he braced for the revelation that it was all some cruel joke, but her lips swept into a smile. An easy, kind one.

"I'm thirsty!" she shouted over the music, and still she sounded muffled.

He nodded, and she pulled him through the dancers, weaving through the choreographed paces. No longer swept up in the dance, he became keenly aware of the sensation of eyes upon his back and how sweaty his palm was. Eirlin didn't seem to notice either of these details.

"Here." She stopped beside the bales of hay lining the clearing. Her chest still heaved from exertion as she smiled at him. "Water or mead?"

"Ah." Leiv circled through the strength of mead, when he had last eaten, how much he had sweat. Eirlin chuckled.

"Come on."

She pulled him away from the longhouse with its mead, to the opposite side of the clearing. Not many people stood near the water, it was early, and most enjoyed the feast. The barrels were placed near the tents to refresh those returning to their homes.

"I could get us some." Eirlin tapped the barrel with her knuckles. "If you let go of my hand."

"Oh." Leiv quickly released her fingers, a blush creeping

up his cheeks. He wiped his palm against his pants and truly hoped she hadn't noticed. Or hadn't cared.

She drew out the ladle and sipped some of the water. He didn't prefer the sting of mead, though he would have drunk it. She was trying, he recognized that, and he wanted to try too.

"You know," she said, as she dipped the ladle back into the barrel. "I was scared when you first came."

"What?" It was an odd confession, and he didn't know how to process it. He didn't immediately take the ladle when she offered it.

"You can't even see that?"

"No, no I can." He grabbed the ladle and drank the water. Admittedly, it had been blurry, but that was unimportant. "You were scared of me?"

"Not of you." She shrugged, taking the ladle and hanging it back over the edge of the barrel. "Of what you represented."

"What do I represent?"

"Change." She leaned against the water barrel and watched the festivities before her. "I don't agree with much of what the capital is doing."

"Why not?"

"Why is it at Kersa?" she asked.

"The… the capital?" he attempted to clarify, not understanding the flow of her logic.

"Yes. Look." She swept her arm over the crowd. "Of all these people, I can count on one hand how many have been to Kersa. But we gather here every single year. Why not here?"

"There are eleven," Leiv mumbled. "At least eleven who have been there."

"The exact number doesn't matter."

"Numbers always matter," he said, and Eirlin laughed. It wasn't the same sardonic laugh as before, and his defense fell. He was used to justifying capital decisions, but he tried to tear aside the callous indifference repetitive arguing had formed and tried to understand. "Why not in Kersa?"

"It's susceptible to attack."

"Any nation should know that to conquer us they'd need to capture Kaighton," he countered. Her face remained stoic, and he knew it was not logic she wanted. "Would you want it here?"

This time, he spread his arm over the scene. She sighed, a small release of breath because, no. No one did.

"I do understand," Leiv began, hesitantly. It felt like a concession, and perhaps it was. Because for all of his time spent in the capital, he did understand Eirlin's fears. "The capital does mean change, but only to protect all this."

Eirlin didn't argue, but she remained stiff at his side. He didn't take it as a slight though, because he had often seen the same reaction. Change was difficult, even when the reason was understood.

"I want to protect this," he said. "That's all I want to do."

She did look at him then, and her eyes were soft instead of icy.

"Eirlin!" a voice cut between them, and Eirlin's gaze tore away. A young woman bounded to her side, wrapping her arms tight around her shoulders, nearly pushing Eirlin over.

"Neta!" Eirlin slapped at the woman's hand, but Neta ignored her.

"I was looking for you!" Neta said, then glanced at Leiv. "Imagine my surprise."

The woman's features were blurry, but he recalled the name and the voice. He had briefly conversed with Neta, a member of the same tribe as Eirlin, and he often saw the two together. She had been pleasant, but now he shifted uncomfortably beneath her perceptive gaze.

"Neta," Eirlin repeated, slapping again at her hand, and this time Neta obliged, removing her arms to slip one through Eirlin's arm.

"Come dance." Neta tugged Eirlin a step away. Leiv stiffened, eyes sweeping over the surroundings, conjuring a mental map of the paths he would need to take to return to Falk's tent.

"Leiv?"

He snapped back to the fire burning bright, the music thrumming loudly, and Eirlin's hand stretched out to him. He looked down at her calloused palm and again wondered why he had taken it in the first place.

Because it felt like home.

"Still need eyes?" Eirlin asked. Leiv looked up to her clear blue eyes, then he took her hand, and they danced.

CHAPTER 10

Eirlin

Leiv was at breakfast, as he had been since his arrival, but this time, Eirlin was uncertain how to approach the empty seat beside her father. Night had a way of skewing events, separating them in time and space, and turning waking memories into dreams. She could conjure the image of his amber eyes outlined with coal, but could almost believe it had been a hallucination fabricated as her mind cycled through all the possible outcomes of her apology.

It would have been easy to believe that lie and slip back to sarcastic comments. It would have been more natural than this hesitation, because she found that after the apology, she didn't know what to do with this man. So foreign, yet so familiar.

Esala sat across from him, and Eirlin watched her sister and wondered at her ability to make anyone at ease. Leiv smiled, and she couldn't fathom what conversation Esala had sparked to elicit such a response. Probably a joke about numbers. She smiled.

"Are you just going to stare at him?" Neta asked. Eirlin jolted, smile sliding into a frown, and she glared at her friend. Neta rolled her eyes. "Come on, you did great yesterday, what do you have left to be nervous about?"

"I'm not nervous," Eirlin muttered. A sly, knowing smile spread across Neta's lips.

"Then stop sulking at the door." Neta looped her arm through Eirlin's and pulled her toward the table. Toward him.

"Good morning!" Neta said, plopping beside Eimon and forcing Eirlin to squeeze between her and Leiv. He shifted on the bench, glancing only momentarily at the two women barging into breakfast. His eyes caught on hers, then turned away.

The unease pressed heavily upon her.

"Morning." Eimon's voice shook with a repressed chuckle. Sitting across from them, Esala glanced between the two suspiciously.

"Good morning," Leiv said.

"I'm surprised to see you here so early, elder," Neta said to Eimon, who laughed. He replied, but Eirlin only heard the rumble of his voice. She glanced at Leiv, who stared at his food. She tried to think of something, anything, to say to him. But when not forming some cold jest, she found she didn't know what to say.

It was easy in the dark of the night, with the thrill of festivities. But here, in the light and bustle of the day, it all felt more uncertain.

"Eirlin?" Esala kicked her boot under the table, and she startled.

"What?"

"Didn't you hear?" A harsh frown tugged at Esala's lips.

"Huh?"

The frown sharpened. "My belt. Father asked about my belt."

"Oh." Eirlin gratefully took the platter Neta passed to her, and focused on the blood pancakes instead of an answer. Though she hadn't heard the question, she knew what it was. "It's almost done."

"Did you dye the beads yourself?" This question came from Leiv, and she gladly took it.

"I did." She turned to him, and he was already looking at her. For a moment she faltered, aware their shoulders touched, so close he would be able to see each expression shifting across her face. The crowded longhouse had never bothered her, until then. "Mostly blue and green. Red is just too difficult."

"There's a way to dye red," Leiv began, voice pitching up with interest, and she smiled at the detail. "In the south, they use—" He stopped, eyes flitting away and brow scrunching, then he looked back, features carefully schooled. "Sorry," he mumbled. "I'm doing it again."

"No!" Eirlin shook her head for emphasis. "No, it's… fine. Maybe a new way to dye red beads would be helpful. I'm slow enough making the belt, I need all the help I can get."

He stared at her, and she grew uncomfortable under his gaze. Perhaps he knew how forced the words had been, when she didn't care what the southerners did with their dye. She busied herself pushing the berries over her pancakes, uncertain if she wanted him to see her clearly.

"It will be done." Esala nudged her with her foot again, and Eirlin glared. "*Before* the ceremony?"

"Of course," Eirlin growled. She wanted to change the conversation, veer it away from the bone belt with its tangle of emotions. She felt frustrated again. It wasn't Esala's fault that she had a belt to sew, that she was awful at sewing, that she hated how the dye stained her fingers as a constant reminder that she was avoiding her duty.

She stood before she recognized she had decided to leave. Neta looked up at her sharply, those too-perceptive eyes once again upon her, and it only stoked the anger.

"Where are you going?" Neta asked.

"To finish a belt," Eirlin grumbled, stepping over the bench, hip bumping against Leiv's shoulder. She didn't look to see his expression, or Esala's, or her father's. She wove through the press of tribesmen, destination set on escaping from the crushing busyness of the longhouse.

As the crisp winter wind rolled over her, the anger shifted back to the familiar unease that hounded her steps, clawed up her ribs, and tightened around her chest. She had fooled herself into thinking a simple apology to Leiv would resolve her unease. The reality was, he had simply been easy to blame, but the true problem didn't lie with him, or even what he represented.

It lay within her.

CHAPTER 11

Leiv

Leiv had almost forgotten about his deadline.

It was the third night after the festival, but still he could feel the phantom impression of Eirlin's fingers entwined with his, pulling him into a dance, settling the sensation of *home* deep within him.

Time only seemed to push the feeling deeper into his core. He had begun to feel at ease in the camp and had forgotten about the snow, blocked roads, and faraway capital.

Merkia gave him tasks to complete, Falk kept him company over lunch, and Esala had an uncanny way of finding him in the evenings and dragging him to the nightly stories around the campfires. She had decided, rightly, that he was fond of stories.

He sat beside her now, but only half-listened to the storyteller as she recounted a tale. He thumbed the edge of his journal, full of numbers. Most he had collected before his glasses had broken, though a few were added with Merkia's help.

Leiv stared down at the black cover and considered the contentment he felt so deeply within. It kept him warm, though the fire was barely large enough to stave off the stinging winter breeze. Two elders sat beside the flames, which brought a larger crowd to listen to the storyteller than usual. Amongst the crowd, he felt like he belonged.

It was what he expected to feel when he arrived in Kaighton, the sensation that had eluded him. But now that he had it, he barely knew what to do with it.

Within a matter of weeks, the tribesmen would break down their tents, and begin the circuit again. They would take their home with them, but he would not. He would leave, alone, to the capital.

A round of applause broke his musings and drew his eyes up from the journal. The storyteller nodded her thanks and accepted a cup of mead. The drink signaled a pause, a respite for the storyteller, and an opportunity for anyone to test their story abilities. The crowd hummed with conversation as they waited for a brave individual to share a tale.

"You should tell one." Esala nudged his arm, and he chuckled at the suggestion. Before he could decline, another spoke.

"Leiv can tell stories." A voice he knew, confident and collected, and he looked across the fire to where she sat beside her father. Her features were a blur, but he saw her straight posture, and the coils of hair escaping her braid. "Esala told me he is a good storyteller."

A nervous twinge pinched his stomach, and he glanced over at Esala, who shrugged with a devious grin.

"It is true," she said.

It made him nervous to be called out to tell a story, and doubly nervous to think of the two sisters discussing him. He traced his thumb over the pages of his journal. A thousand tales flitted through his mind, all memories in his mother's voice.

"Tell us a tale," Eirlin prompted, and he looked back to the dark smudge in his vision. The crowd waited for his response, but he was caught for a moment wondering what expression was on her face.

After the dance, he didn't know what to expect from her.

"Alright," he said. One tale caught in his mind, one that reminded him of her resilient ice eyes. The crowd quieted, pulling their furs tighter against the cold. The storyteller sipped her mead, then dipped her head in acknowledgment, allowing the start of his story.

"Late one winter night," he began, but the refrain felt odd on his tongue. Not unpleasant, but awkward when he had only spoken those words aloud to children. "A young woman went hunting for a white wolf," he continued, and there was a murmur of recognition. It was an old tale, but one with three different endings decided based on how the teller felt. "She packed only three things with her: a silver dagger, a silk net, and golden lichen.

"She trekked three long days in snow from three days fall. Uphill, downhill, over river, through forest, until she found the tracks of the white wolf. For three more days, she followed the tracks, never veering as she searched for the wolf. This wolf, it was told, could grant the wish of any who captured it, and this young warrior desperately wanted one wish."

Leiv paused. A log popped in a burst of sparks, and a mother readjusted a fussy baby. He let the pause lengthen, just a bit more, as his mother always had. It gave the listeners time to think what their wish would be, she had told him.

"At the end of the third day of tracking, she found the burrow of the white wolf. She spread her net in the snow and waited. For three days and three nights, she waited, until the wolf emerged. He stepped into her trap, and though he raged, he was unable to escape. After a time, when the wolf had settled, the woman approached."

"'You have bested me,' the wolf told her. 'Release me, and I will grant you one wish.'" Leiv deepened his voice for the wolf's words, but couldn't look at the blurred figures around the campfire as he did. His mother always gave the characters their distinct voices, but it felt awkward when he was the one performing.

He paused again, longer this time, letting the audience squirm as they awaited which end he would choose. Hopeful, despondent, or malicious.

"The warrior said, 'No.'" Leiv spoke each word slowly, and the audience leaned in closer. With his words, he had avoided the malicious end, but two possibilities remained. Hopeful. Despondent.

"'I want two wishes,' she said. 'I will not let you go free until I receive two.' The wolf laughed and said, 'I would rather die than give you two!' But the woman confidently said, 'I will free you, and I will feed you, and I will care for you. Then you will grant me two wishes.'"

Hopeful.

"The wolf, shocked by her courage, howled with laughter and said, 'Daughter of man, I accept your terms.' She cut his bonds, trusting him to speak the truth, fed him the lichen, and he granted her two wishes."

The story never described what she wished for; a mystery for the hearers to determine. But the story ended with a promise, a future.

"Thus ends the tale."

The moment broke, and there was polite applause before the crowd turned to each other to discuss what wishes they would ask for. He blinked, eyes stinging from staring at the flames, and he looked over the crowd, heart beating wildly in his chest.

"That was good." Eirlin appeared at his side, shoulder brushing against his as she sat.

"I told you." Esala grinned.

"My mother was a storyteller," he explained, but saying it out loud tightened his throat, and he looked down at the journal clutched in his hands. "She told me many."

"She was a good storyteller." There was a pause, then slowly, carefully, Eirlin asked, "What happened?"

"The plague." There was no reason to hide it, it wasn't a secret. It was simply what happened, but it was hard, it was personal, and it hurt. "It took them both."

"I'm so sorry," Esala murmured.

"The plague," Eirlin repeated. From the corner of his eyes, he could see her squint at him. "You would have been young."

"I was. I'd only just received my belt." He turned the journal over in his hands, feeling the need to do something as she stared at him. "That was when I went to the capital to live with my uncle."

"And you still remember her stories?"

"Of course." He looked up, with a gentle smile. "I won't ever be able to forget."

She smiled back at him, a small, sad one that spoke of an understanding. She knew the pain, more than he cared to admit. It was an awkward recognition that they were similar. With the understanding came uncertainty. Her eyes flitted over his face, perhaps thinking the same thing.

"I'm sorry for your loss," she said, words he had given to her father. "And thank you, for telling the story."

She stood, face blurring so he couldn't distinguish her expression, and she left before he could thank her for asking for a story. He was glad she had. Speaking the familiar words was a reminder of what he missed when he moved from the tribe to a sedentary life in the capital.

It pressed the warm feeling of home deeper and sharpened the uncertainty of what he should do with that sensation.

CHAPTER 12

Eirlin

The small bone beads were tiresome to thread, and the tough leather made each take a painstaking amount of effort to cinch into place. Eirlin had to carefully place each blue, green, red, and white bead to replicate the design handed down to the sisters through their mother's line.

A blue bead. A green bead. She placed each with painstaking effort, and when a full block of color emerged, Eirlin kissed the completed section. It was custom, to imbue the belt with all the love of the family, but Eirlin would have kissed the beads simply grateful to see progress.

She sat hunched in the daylight, cheeks red with cold, but enjoying every drop of sunlight. In the tent behind her, Neta's mother separated clothes for mending, while her daughters scurried about to complete whatever task their mother handed down. Eirlin had come to their tent to keep away from the silence of her own.

Around her, the camp bustled, and she listened to it to keep her mind from wandering. Occasionally, a group of workers would pass, and she would overhear snippets of their conversations.

"Kina is about ready to have her fourth…"

"… fork of the Goresh, heard there was good fishing…"

"…wolves spotted on the westward side, the cold brings them down…"

"What do you think?"

Eirlin belatedly realized the last question had been asked of her. She looked up from the beads to her sister squatting at her side.

"Well?"

"What was the question?" Eirlin welcomed the pause, letting the needle stay half-stuck in the leather, and flexed her fingers.

"The reindeer!" Esala exclaimed. There was a spark in her eyes, and though she searched, Eirlin could find no trace of sickness in them. "Can I feed them? I haven't seen them in so long!"

"No," Eirlin said curtly, then folded back over the belt, her own pressing uncomfortably into her stomach. "I already fed them today, and I can't go with you. I promise you, they won't care if you come back today or tomorrow."

"Yes, they will," Esala moped. "I could go by myself."

"I heard wolves were spotted." Eirlin refused to look into her sister's large, hopeful eyes.

"By Krissen." Esala scoffed. She ran a finger over a finished section of beads, managing to find a loose thread, and tugged at it. "He's hardly reliable."

"Stop that." Eirlin waved aside her hand, but couldn't help but chuckle at her retort. Krissen wasn't a grounded storyteller. "Why don't you ask father to go with you?"

"He's too busy being an elder." Esala sighed. "Why can't you come?"

With a flourish, Eirlin swept her hand over the unbeaded section of the belt.

"You still have that much left?" Esala gasped. "You're slow!"

"I know, I know," Eirlin grumbled. Her mother had been an excellent seamstress, which meant Eirlin never developed the skill. It was easier to pass what needed mending to her willing mother. "Just leave me to it, it will be done eventually."

Surprisingly, her sister complied, sulking off, probably to go bother their father once again. With the distraction gone, Eirlin slipped back into the monotony of her chore, able to empty her mind and simply listen to the voices around her.

Until she heard his voice.

Always even, always succinct. At the sound, her eyes flicked up, and she caught sight of him down the road, speaking with another man. Her eyes fell back to focus on the leather between her hands, the needle, the bone beads.

A blue bead. A red bead.

It was hard to concentrate when his voice tingled at the back of her mind, conjuring thoughts of his hand pressed into hers and the lilt of his voice as he told the story the previous night; a story from his mother. She couldn't help how the thought curved a smile on her lips.

His parents had passed ten years prior, during the plague, and still he remembered them so fondly. *'I won't ever be able to forget,'* he had said, and she immediately knew he understood.

It felt wrong to feel the pain of her mother's loss when it was already three years past, and everyone else seemed to have grown used to her absence. She had tried to smother the grief until it was nothing but numbness in the periphery of her consciousness. But then, Leiv had told the story, and his smile had been tinged with sadness. Even after ten years.

Eirlin's hand paused, and she stared down at the belt, the one her mother should have been making for Esala.

She wanted to think it was the changes the capital implemented that caused her frustration with Leiv, but she knew that wasn't true. She feared the change, but it wasn't because of what would come, but because what was being left behind. She desperately clung to a time from before, a time when her mother was alive. But it was foolish to think nothing would change.

Esala's belt would be completed, and she would go through the coming-of-age ceremony as Eirlin had, as their mother had. That wouldn't change. Anything the capital introduced wouldn't deter their traditions, and wouldn't erase the memories of all who had come before.

Not of Leiv's parents. Not of her mother.

Perhaps, though frightening, they could move forward, create change honoring the memory of those who had passed, and create a future guarding what was most important. Eirlin suspected that was what Leiv understood all along.

"Still not done?" Neta crashed down at her side, all smiles and the faint scent of juniper from the branches her mother had sent her to gather for brooms.

"No." Eirlin rubbed her eyes to clear away her convoluted thoughts. It was too much. She wondered if Leiv felt tired after his mental work.

"You have two weeks left." Neta rested her head against Eirlin's shoulder. "Don't worry, you'll make it."

"If I have enough beads," Eirlin muttered, flicking her basket. She had a secret fear she would be nearly finished, only to find she had no suitable beads left. She had counted, over and over, but the beads looked oddly lacking in their basket.

"You'll have enough," Neta said.

"Enough of what?" His boots crunched into the snow beside the overhang. With a quick, steadying breath, Eirlin smiled up at him.

"Of course, you would appear when numbers are mentioned," she quipped. "Do they summon you?"

He laughed; a pleasant sound, like rain in spring.

"The beads," Neta said. He looked down at the belt in Eirlin's lap, then knelt before the basket. He plucked a single bead from amongst its brethren, and considered the smooth blue bone, before squinting at the rest.

"You disappeared," a red-haired man huffed as he crunched up beside Leiv. "What are you doing?"

"Counting, obviously." Neta chuckled, straightening off of Eirlin's shoulder. "You're the one he's been staying with, right?"

"I am. Falk, of the Lantri tribe."

"Eirlin, of tribe Kani."

"Neta, of tribe Kani," Neta said, then added, "You're betrothed to Krissi, correct?"

His cheeks reddened to match his hair. "How do you know that?"

"I know her cousin." Neta shrugged. "We've talked."

"Neta knows everyone," Eirlin explained, then stole a glance at Leiv, who still hunched over her basket. His eyes flicked briefly to the spare space on the belt. A shiver ran down her spine. She felt awkward with her work under his intense consideration.

"We are betrothed," Falk said, voice strengthened as the moment of shyness passed. He grabbed Leiv's shoulder and hauled him back to his feet. "Which is exactly why we need to go. The only reason I'm here and not with her is because this one insists he doesn't want to walk to Merkia's tent alone. How did you even end up helping in Kani?"

Eirlin and Leiv's eyes caught in a quick, furtive glance.

"Though, it seems you're perfectly fine wandering off now," Falk continued with a sigh.

"I didn't wander off." Leiv rolled the blue bead around his palm, then dropped it back into the basket. "I heard their voices, I knew where they were."

Falk humphed and trudged off, waving Leiv to follow. "If my betrothal is broken, it's your fault."

"Neta, Eirlin." Leiv dipped his head before following Falk. There was the exchange of jokes, his laughter once again, then they blended into the crowd, and she could no longer distinguish his voice. Like he had hers.

Eirlin tugged the thread tightly. Too tightly.

"It's too bad." Neta sighed.

"What is?" Eirlin asked, to oblige Neta's incessant desire to talk.

"That he's going to be leaving so soon."

She paused. "Soon?"

"Probably by the end of the week," Neta said smoothly,

then shrugged. "If the weather holds."
    "Oh."

CHAPTER 13

Leiv

"Shouldn't you be escorting me?" Merkia grumbled, but he was learning that her complaints held little weight. He began to think of it less as grumbling, and more as her version of small talk.

"If you're not a grandma"—he offered her his arm—"why would you need an escort?"

She looked at him with a thin, skeptical smile. His jest was familiar, and he wondered if he had assumed too much of their new relationship. He had simply felt comfortable. But then she wrapped her arm around his, and the surge of nervousness just as quickly abated.

"Hmph. At least I am the one with the eyes of a youth."

He grinned but had no rebuttal. She had requested he fetch more pouches for the herbs, but in the end, she consented to go with him when his apprehensive directional questions became too tiring.

They walked along the path with comfortable silence between them, her leading and him allowing her to pull him along in her surprisingly strong grip. A fiery sunset streaked across the pale sky. With dusk closing in, the camp readied for the long darkness with a rush of activity he could easily get lost in.

"When you leave," Merkia said suddenly. At the words, his throat tightened, and it was a little harder to breathe. "What will you do with all your information about the herbs?"

He glanced down at her sharp silver eyes, and he suspected she wasn't asking about the herbs.

"You were thinking about it, weren't you?" she prodded. "Your departure?"

"No," he said, but looked away to the blobs of shapes around them. "It wasn't that.

He had been distracted that afternoon; she had to remind him which herb needed to be sorted three separate times. But he hadn't been thinking about his eventual departure, he had managed to let that sink so far to the back of his mind he had nearly forgotten.

Remembering stung.

He'd been thinking about bone beads.

"Merkia," he started, tentatively, "how long does it take to dye beads?"

"A day or two." Merkia shrugged, shoulder slipping up and down against his arm. "Depends. Why are you thinking about beads?"

"I want to try dyeing some," he said simply, words vague. It felt wrong to admit Eirlin needed more, but by his estimation, she was lacking. He hesitated, afraid to invite Merkia's scrutinizing silver eyes upon him at the mention of Eirlin's name. So instead, he said, "I want to try a different dyeing method."

"Hmm," she mumbled. "Where are you getting the bone?"

"I… hadn't thought of that."

"Ha!" She shook her head but patted his hand. "I'll get you some. Stay here."

"What?" He halted as she pulled her guiding arm away. "Now?"

"Boy, can't you see?" She scoffed, her form blurring as she tramped further away. "We're in the middle of the Exchange!"

He, in fact, could not see. The Exchange was an open square of stalls situated on the opposite end of the camp from the longhouse, where tribesmen could exchange goods. Leiv had visited when he first arrived, but without his glasses, it was simply too overwhelming a place. He hadn't noticed when they'd entered, too used to simply ignoring the blur surrounding him and focusing instead on the small circle of the world he could see.

Now that he acknowledged the outside world, the busyness of the space was overwhelming.

Merkia slipped out of his view, and he shifted uncomfortably. Tribesmen moved around him, and he stepped back into the entrance of a row of tents to move out of their way.

Instead of watching the confusing blur before him, he looked down the still pathway. At the end of the path, he could discern the outline of a fence but, though he squinted, he couldn't see any dark forms of reindeer. A figure swept across his vision, with the snap of a long black braid and the jingle of sleigh bells.

His feet crunched through the snow, and he turned the corner to see the figure follow the curve of the fence.

"Hey," he called, wondering, hoping, but not certain. She paused, turned, and he knew he was wrong. Too slim, too short. "Esala?"

"Hello, Leiv!" She sounded chipper, but her figure didn't stop shifting.

"Where are you going?"

There was a beat of hesitation before she said, "Are you with Eirlin?"

"No," he said quickly and wondered why she would think he was. "Why?"

"Oh, nothing, it's just…" Another hesitation, then a heaved sigh. "I'm going to care for the reindeer, and she's been overprotective."

"Why is that?"

"Because I was sick," Esala muttered. But then she added in a softer tone, "Like our mother."

"Oh." He faltered at the mention of their mother. He knew what it was like to lose a parent. But unlike the sisters, he had no siblings. The closest he had to a sibling had been Forinth, who had also been taken by the plague. He wondered what it would feel like to so desperately want to protect another.

The thought of Eirlin's concern perked the corner of his lips.

"She doesn't think I should care for the reindeer yet," Esala continued, voice tentative at his pause.

"Should you?"

"Does it look like I'm still sick?" she asked.

"I don't think so." He chuckled and heard the girl laugh. "Just be careful, it's getting dark."

"Don't you be overprotective too!" she called back. The words were meant to chide, but they warmed his chest. With a jingle, Esala pulled the sled further from the camp, and Leiv walked back to the entrance of the tent row. Merkia had not yet returned, but he thought he caught sight of her short silhouette chatting at a nearby stall.

A smile still curved upon his lips, until a passing man said, "Wolves!"

"Not just Krissen's report. Cove confirmed it as well."

The pair walked past, but Leiv turned his head to follow them, straining to hear their words over the din of the Exchange.

"Cove? Still, I can't imagine them being this close to camp."

"The winter has been cold; it brings them down from the high north."

The conversation continued, but Leiv lost the words to distance. He had heard the rumors but hadn't taken much interest in them. He had no reindeer to watch and no reason to venture toward the fringes of the camp.

Like Esala had just done.

He glanced back to the shape he thought was Merkia, but the figure had disappeared. For a moment, his head swiveled between where he'd last seen Merkia and Esala. Then, he turned and marched toward the fence.

After sunset, the world darkened quickly, only more pronounced by his lack of clear vision, but he followed the fence and hoped Esala had not diverged from its lead. The cold air stung his lungs, but he persisted forward. He tried to reason that he was being irrational, but the rumor circled in his head, and he assured himself that Merkia would understand why he left.

The fence curved away from the tents, swinging closer to the foreboding line of conifers. The snow was hard-packed from frequent sled traffic, and ahead, he saw the golden glow of a lantern beside a cluster of large dark shapes. His pace quickened, and relief cooled his worry as her features grew more defined with each step nearer. Then she looked up, and her features morphed into confusion.

"Leiv?" she asked as she dumped one of the skins of water into the trough. "What are you doing?"

He leaned against the railing, sucking in great breaths of air. A curious muzzle snuffed at the back of his head, searching for something good to eat; lichen or a bit of salt.

"I just…" He shook his head, feeling rather silly as he stood there. "I heard rumors about wolves. I got… worried."

"Oh!" Esala chuckled. "Would wolves come this close to camp?"

"I don't know." His cheeks burned as she laughed. "But we're not that close to camp."

He looked back toward the Karish camp, but the individual tents had merged into one thick line cutting across his vision.

"Thank you," Esala said and dumped another skin into the trough. Leiv leaned his head against the board and sighed.

"Merkia will scold me."

"Oh, she will too!" the girl said with a chuckle. She set the second skin back on the sled and slipped a knife from her belt.

Leiv heaved off the fence, and as she cut the strings of the square bales, he hauled the hay through the fence slats.

"What do you do in the capital?" Esala asked. He jolted at the question, losing a bit of hay on the snow before he forced himself back into the familiar rhythm of caring for the reindeer.

"I…" He grabbed another handful and tried to hide the disquiet the question produced. "I sort through a lot of information. Statistics and such."

"Hmm, no." Esala cut the last string and slipped the knife back into its sheath. "I mean, apart from your counting."

"That's mostly all I do." Leiv shoved more hay through and watched the reindeer hungrily nose through their food. "Sometimes we gather to tell stories, and we do celebrate the festivals, it's just a little different."

"It seems lonely."

It was.

"What I do is important." Leiv wiped the dust of hay off his coat and avoided looking over at the girl. "Someone has to make that sacrifice."

"Still," she murmured. "It sounds lonely."

She was right, and he said nothing more. As they stood in silence, a reindeer lifted its head, ears perked. Another followed suit, then stamped its foot. Together, the small herd abandoned the hay and shifted backward, away from the fence.

Leiv stiffened, turning sharply to the woods. He scanned the forest line, seeking what the reindeer had sensed. Esala lurched forward, grabbing his hand.

"Leiv," she hissed and pointed. He followed her direction and saw them; small dark shapes separating from the line of trees. The wolves paused on the snow, before one slunk slowly forward.

"Run to the camp," Leiv ordered, pushing Esala backward.

"But—"

"Run!"

CHAPTER 14

Eirlin

When Eimon returned to their tent, Eirlin didn't even mind that he came with chores, she was just content to no longer be alone with her thoughts. They looped in a simple, aggravating circle: change made her uneasy, Leiv brought change, but perhaps it was good change, but what would change when he left.

The pang of disappointment she had felt at Neta's off-handed comment still brought a heat up her neck and into her cheeks.

"Here," she offered, taking the bulk of the fur her father hauled in. He mumbled a *thank you*, nearly lost beneath the pile. "These need to be sewn, don't they?"

He chuckled, dropping his armload onto the bed the girls shared. Eirlin heaved a sigh; she would be glad to not see a needle and thread for ages.

"These furs are for the candidates." Eimon lifted one pelt, the small white one of a rabbit.

"Oh." Eirlin looked down at the furs still in her arms, feeling their weight.

"You could still be counted as one," her father said gently.

Another sigh and she dropped her armload on the bed and sat beside them. She fiddled with a soft fox tail and worked through a new circle of conflicting thoughts.

"Do you…" She paused, burying her hand deep into the pile of soft pelts. "Do you think I'm ready?"

"I wouldn't have offered you to join otherwise." Eimon sat at her side. He still held the white pelt, thumb circling through the fur.

"Even after everything?" She looked away from his hands, to where her own disappeared before her.

"Everything?"

"With Leiv." Her voice was a whisper. *Builds us up*, her father had said. But while Leiv strove to protect them, she had simply been destructive. It was shameful; behavior not fitting for a candidate.

"Little songbird," he breathed, but this time she smiled at the nickname. "No one is perfect, I don't expect perfection. You may have acted wrong, but you did apologize, and that takes perhaps more strength."

The world blurred as the tears brimmed in her eyes. It made her think of Leiv, of his eyes, of honey. She swiped the tears away with the back of her hand, clearing her vision.

"I would like to be counted," she said, and he smiled.

"You will do well." He pressed a kiss to her forehead. "My little songbird."

The unease hounding her for weeks finally, finally receded. As the warmth of her father's kiss washed over her, she felt her ribs relax and expand, her shoulders slump, and the tension throughout her body slide away.

Change was coming, but it would not destroy.

Just as the warmth settled into her body, a cry wound through the camp. At first, it was only a rustle, a nudge to wake from the reverie of sleep, and it was easily cast aside. But it grew, more voices joining in, and it was impossible to ignore.

"Wolves!"

Not a rumor. Eirlin stiffened and looked up at her father. He held her gaze, and she knew he thought the same thing.

Esala.

"Eirlin," her father began, but she was already standing, already tugging on her boots.

"Where is she?" she demanded. He started lacing his boots, and her heart doubled its pace. She burst from the tent, eyes scanning the camp. People gathered outside their tents, passing hushed gossip. Then she caught sight of a man slinging a quiver around his chest, and she rushed after him.

The man was faster, and she began to fall behind. She strained her eyes in the darkness to keep sight of his figure until she realized he ran toward the pens. She pressed her legs as fast as she could as she ran to the fence line.

Down the fence, she ran, though her lungs ached, though her legs burned. She followed the man with the quiver as more men with weapons joined him.

Esala had not returned home. It had already been suspicious, but Eilrin had passed it off and assumed she had simply lost track of time listening to stories.

The snow glowed brightly with the light of the gibbous moon, and ahead, men stood starkly contrasted on the plane of white. She set her course toward the group and ignored the shouts of warning. Then a hand grabbed her arm. She tried to wrench away but rammed against the fence. Pain sliced sharply up her side.

"Eirlin." Her father gasped, heaving breaths as he stood at her side, hand still wrapped around her forearm. "Wait."

A bow string snapped and her gaze tore from her father to where a few paces ahead, an archer released his arrow.

It *thunked* into a large canine.

A wolf.

The beast yelped and collapsed, blood staining the white snow crimson. The sight roiled Eirlin's stomach.

More wolves prowled, though they eyed the approaching torchlight warily. Eirlin's gaze bounced over each, silently counting as she searched. Then found what she was looking for. Two shapes forged ahead, rushing to meet the torches of the camp. One tall, one short, then they entered the glow of the torchlight, and Eirlin's breath hitched.

Leiv, dragging Esala with him.

Another arrow, but this one buried helplessly into the snow. Another, hitting a wolf which yipped and turned away.

One step, then another, until her sister and the census taker burst into the circle of the tribesmen with their bows and collapsed onto the snow.

"Forward!" a man shouted, and the archers advanced, chasing back the wolves.

Eirlin rushed forward, and her father let her. She fell to the ground, clutching at her sister's hair, her cheeks, pressing her forehead against her own.

"What were you doing?" Eirlin couldn't help the angry roar that tore from her body. Her heart pounded too loud, too fast, but she couldn't slow it, not when her lungs ached and her fingers quaked, and Esala was before her in the same state.

"I'm sorry," she rasped.

"What were you thinking!"

"I'm sorry." But it wasn't Esala who responded this time. She looked over to Leiv, kneeling at Esala's side, staring down at his hands splayed across the snow. "I shouldn't have let her go."

Eirlin just looked at him. There was a thin cut on his cheek, and blood slipped down his jaw. Her grip around Esala tightened, and she opened her mouth, but tears rolled down his face, mingling with the blood, and she didn't know the words to comfort them both.

"It's okay." Her father's heavy hand fell upon Leiv's shoulder, firm and gentle. He didn't look up. "It's okay."

But it wasn't okay, and he wasn't okay.

Esala's arms finally slipped around Eirlin's chest, and she held her sister even tighter. Eirlin hadn't thought to don her coat, and now, sitting in the snow, the chill began to work up her legs, to her very core.

Tears still slipped down Leiv's cheeks.

"Come," Eimon ordered. "To the longhouse."

CHAPTER 15

Leiv

L eiv shivered. Though he sat on the warm stones of the hearth with the licking flames at his back, he still felt cold. Merkia sat beside him, preparing a salve for his cheek.

"How many were there?" Veight asked, for the fourth time. Leiv tried to conjure the number that should have been in his mind. He couldn't remember if he had counted the wolves. He couldn't remember what his last answer had been.

"I don't remember," he murmured.

"You said twelve, correct?" another elder pressed. "Correct?"

Leiv bit his cheek, trying to think, but it pulled at the raw wound and he winced.

"Enough," Merkia chided. "He said thirteen wolves, then ten. Do with that what you will. Now, shoo! Let me tend his wound in peace."

She flapped her hand at the men, and they moved back to the table where the other seven elders sat to discuss the insufficient information. They debated how best to protect the reindeer and the camp, but their voices were a drone in his ears. All he saw was the flash of fangs. All he heard was the crack of glass shattering on the skull of a large, gray wolf.

"Thank you," he mumbled.

"Ha!" Merkia dabbed the green ointment against the cut, where a fragment of lantern glass had sliced his flesh. "Abandoning me, then forcing me out of my warm tent?"

She clucked her tongue, but there was no chastisement in her tone. "Next time you try heroics, make sure it's in daylight so I don't have to traipse around in the dark."

Merkia wiped her hand on her apron, then stood. She laid a motherly hand against his jaw, before walking away to clean her instruments.

"There were fourteen." Leiv glanced over to where Eirlin sat on the hearth. "I counted."

He stared at her, at the way the firelight shaded her jaw and warmed her skin. Esala mumbled in her sleep, and his gaze dropped to her stretched between them, feet against Leiv's thigh, head in Eirlin's lap. Absently, Eirlin slipped her fingers through her sister's unbraided hair.

Eirlin loved her sister. Seeing the two together, it never seemed so simple. In the capital, there was a way of making things so complex and convoluted. *He* had a way of making things complex and convoluted.

Sometimes, the simplest things in life were easy to overlook. Things of love and sacrifice. Both things the cold north had a way of bringing to the forefront.

The simple truth was that he wanted a home.

"I'll make sure they get the right number." She turned from watching the elders, and he snapped his gaze up to meet hers. She sat just far enough that her features were cloudy, and he was afraid he missed something in her expression. Something important, something that would explain the tightening of his chest.

"Thank you," she said. "For protecting her."

"I…" he started, looking down at his boots. "I didn't do much."

"You tried."

He didn't feel like he had done anything. He had been afraid. The only reason he and Esala sat before the fire now was because of the archers. The thought deepened the chill in his bones, and he shivered.

The benches groaned as the elders rose, adjourning for the evening.

"Well." Eimon sighed as he approached the three. His eyes caught on his younger daughter. "That was unpleasant business. The winter was harsh, the wolves hungry. That's all we can surmise."

Leiv and Eirlin said nothing.

"Hmm." The elder rubbed his beard, then scooped up Esala. "I will take her back." Before he turned to leave, he looked down at Leiv. His usually open and friendly face had grown stiff with a heavy seriousness. Leiv straightened. "You have all my thanks."

The elder left before Leiv could point out that he hadn't

done much, that he had been the one to let Esala go unquestioned into the darkening night.

You tried.

Leiv and Eirlin still sat before the fire. Neither moved, and he grew uncomfortable at her side. He glanced over, but she watched her father leave. Her face had also transformed into something deeper, something more serious.

The north drew out simple things, and he found he was nervous to know what a few wolves would reveal.

"We should—" Leiv rose, but Eirlin caught his hand before he could step away.

"Wait." She paused, looked at their hands, then said, "Can I speak with you?"

CHAPTER 16
Eirlin

"Here." Eirlin set the mug on the table before Leiv.

With the elders gone, the only other tribesmen in the longhouse were the few women preparing food for the next day, whispering of the recent events and sneaking glances at the two at the table. In the flickering firelight, the salve Merkia applied to the cut on his cheek made the skin sickly green. Leiv seemed more tired than he had ever before, and it took him too long to reach for the tea.

"To calm your nerves," she added when his fingers finally slipped around the mug.

"That obvious?" He chuckled.

"Well." Eirlin sat down across from him. "You were attacked by a wolf, I wouldn't be surprised if you trekked through the snow all by yourself to get out of here tomorrow."

Leiv was silent, and she peeked up at him from her mug. He studied the tea, brow furrowed, and she wondered if he calculated how many leaves she had used from their stores to make it. With the crease between his eyes, he looked more like himself and less like the shaken man kneeling in the snow.

"No," he said, with a force that startled her. "No, I disagree."

"With what?" Eirlin asked, defensive at such a forceful reaction.

"I don't want to leave." He looked up, honey gaze latching onto hers.

"Even if a wolf wants you for dinner?" She tried a smile, but it felt forced, so she dropped it and met his serious gaze.

"Even so." His fingers tightened around the mug. "The simplest things reveal the greatest truths."

"What do you mean?"

"You love your sister," he said, and she nodded. "You know who you love, you know who you want to protect. It's so simple."

Eirlin pictured her sister in the snow and knew she would have done anything to protect the girl. It *was* simple. She would give her own life to protect her sister.

"I missed that simplicity in the city," he continued, finding the understanding in her softening gaze. "Here, it's easy to remember why I'm working so hard to preserve all of this."

"You're leaving soon," she murmured, then bit her tongue and regretted the words. A forlorn smile twisted the corner of his lips.

"So I am." He sighed, looking back down at the mug between his hands.

He spoke of the simpleness of things, but sitting across from him, she found nothing was simple. Her mother was still gone, a hard road of change lay ahead, and this confusing man sat before her.

In the silence, there were many words she could say. Right ones and wrong ones, and one that would lead to even more uncertainties. It was easier when she held him away, easier than trying to understand him. Easier when she didn't think about him, kneeling in the snow with apologies on his lips, when all she wanted to do was wrap him in her arms and thank him, thank him, thank him.

He looked up eventually after the silence had long run its course.

"What did you want to sa—"

"Why don't you stay?"

His mouth was still open mid-word, but his breath hitched and they entered back into that silence.

"I…" he tried, but failed. He studied the drink he hadn't touched. "If I don't go back, I won't be able to show the capital how we can use the numbers. If we can use it… we could protect ourselves. Even better than we already can."

"What about you?" she pressed, though his shoulders hunched. "What do you want?"

"I want everyone to be safe."

"I see." It was what she wanted too, but that was not what she wanted to hear from him now. "Well, thank you, again. For protecting my sister."

"I—" he started, but she heard the deflection in his tone

and narrowed her eyes sharply. He faltered, eyes widening at the anger in her expression.

"No," she said sternly. "You protected her, a noble thing to do, and I am forever indebted to you for doing so."

His lips parted, then closed. Finally, he said, "Thank you."

"Now, drink that," she ordered as she stood, stabbing a finger toward the mug. "It's a secret blend from my mother, with some hard-to-find ingredients, so you better drink it all."

Eirlin turned before he could see the smile on her lips. She didn't want him to see the sadness at the edges of the expression, because against all rationale, she didn't want him to go.

She really was bad at change.

CHAPTER 17

Leiv

"It's just shock," Merkia said, but it didn't feel like *just shock*. He felt cold, down to his core, and he even added an extra fur vest to his usual clothes. Merkia saw how his lips twisted into a frown and rolled her eyes. "So you can fight with a wolf, but the thought of it makes you squeamish?"

He cinched a pouch of dried thyme, still frowning.

"Fine." The grandma sighed, plucking the pouch from his hand. "I prescribe tea. Drink tea, it's a cure-all."

She was pandering to him, smirking as he glowered at her.

It wasn't just shock. He knew the cause, though he was hesitant to acknowledge the truth sulking in his mind.

It wasn't the wolf that bothered him.

It was his impending departure.

The wolf was a small part of the tribe's life, already a rumor twisted beyond recognition as it passed through the camp. Within a fortnight, a new tale would replace it, then another, and another. They would break camp, part ways, and begin their circuits for another nine months. More tales would be told of wolves, foxes, and bears.

But for Leiv, that wolf would be the only he would encounter. He would return to the capital with its two-story buildings and dirt roads, to his single-room apartment, to the stacks of paper to file away.

'Why don't you stay?'

He picked up a brittle thyme branch and twirled it between his fingers, focusing on the feel of the twist of the stem, on what was real. Her voice was a tantalizing whisper in his mind, beckoning him to think, to consider, to imagine that staying was a possibility.

His task was collecting numbers, he reminded himself. He wasn't bitter. He would turn all the information into something that could protect his people. If that meant he didn't get to travel the circuit with them, so be it.

But he wanted a home.

"Leiv!" Eimon burst into the tent. Leiv shifted his gaze from the crisp leaves to the vague outline. He thought he saw the elder wave his hand. "Come, you will be glad to see this!"

"Taking away my help?" Merkia huffed.

Leiv placed the branch onto the table and slowly stood. He knew what the elder had to show him, and was not surprised when he stepped out of the tent and saw the tall, brawny form of Kreilen.

"Leiv!" the wagon driver exclaimed, pulling him into an iron-grip hug. "All in one piece, I see!"

"Kreilen," Leiv said evenly, not to betray the pang of disappointment. "It's good to see you."

It was. Kreilen was a kind man, long-suffering in all of Leiv's travels. But his presence inevitably meant departure.

"You finally made it." Leiv forced his voice to sound light and joking.

"Finally indeed." Krielen released Leiv with a laugh. "The capital should reconsider a wagon. Sure, they're fine in Kersa, but out here?"

"Don't worry yourself over it." Eimon chuckled. "We have a large tankard of mead that's been waiting for you."

"Perfect. With that, I'll be ready to leave by tomorrow before any more snow can come!" Kreilen clapped Leiv heavily on the shoulder. He swayed beneath the bear of a man's grip, not immediately replying. Kreilen's eyebrows shot up. "You don't want to leave now, do you?"

"No," Leiv quickly replied, and the man released a relieved breath.

"Oh, good. I know you're obsessed with those deadlines, but that would've been a bit too much. What's another day on a missed deadline, anyway?"

"No," Leiv repeated, and with the word, he made a rash decision. "There's one last thing I need to do."

"Good. Then I'm going to get that tankard. But before that." Kreilen slipped his hand from Leiv's shoulder to a pocket of his coat. From within, he pulled a small wooden box. Leiv's heart skipped at the sight of it.

"Glasses?" he asked, eagerly taking the box. He flipped open the lid and found exactly that. A neat pair of thin wire-rimmed glasses. "How did you know?"

"A little bird." Kreilen winked. "Our elders aren't ones to let their people suffer."

"Thank you both." Leiv reverently took the glasses from the case and slipped them into place. The world snapped to crisp focus, the blurry background transforming into the fibrous cords of ropes staked to the ground, the fur-lined hoods of coats, and the glinting metal of sleigh bells. The wireframes pressed cold against his skin, an odd sensation after such an extended time without them.

"Thank you," Leiv repeated.

"Back as you should be." Kreilen chuckled.

"Join us when Merkia releases you," Eimon said. Leiv nodded, waving goodbye as the two men began toward the longhouse.

"Hmph." Merkia squinted at him when he returned to the tent. "You look quite formal now."

"Grandma," he said before he could stop himself. Rash, he reminded himself, but the idea had rooted in his mind, and he couldn't shake it. "Can I have your help?"

"With what?" Her eyebrow lifted with muffled bemusement at his serious tone.

"Words."

A smile quirked her lips. "You may have asked the wrong person."

He shrugged. Anyone was better than just him. He had never been good with words, always too calculated, always turning over every possible meaning, always trying to be too exact.

Her words were confident, clear and crisp, like the winter wind. When he thought of the stray curls of her braid, her calloused palms, and her resilient ice-blue eyes, his words just tumbled apart all over again.

But he would find the words to say. Her question looped in his mind, and he could not stop thinking through the possibilities. It was an impulsive hope pushing him forward, but the more he dwelled on the possibility, the more warmth spread through his chest.

He wanted a home.

Merkia smiled, then nodded. "I will help."

CHAPTER 18

Eirlin

E irlin knew Kreilen had come for Leiv.

She ignored the fact. Ignored it, because she wanted to ignore the rest of the thoughts swirling in her mind when she thought of that man. That man, and the ridiculous question she had asked him.

Instead, she bent over the belt, intent on finishing it before the ceremony. The closer she came to the deadline, the more she became certain she didn't have enough beads to finish. She pulled a thread tight and it snapped. She hissed in frustration as she snatched the freed white bead before losing sight of it in the snow.

"Are you alright?"

She stared up at the man standing in front of her before recognition set in. Leiv. Glasses perched on his nose, and through them, his honey-brown eyes seemed slightly larger.

"What?" he asked, and only then did she realize she had been staring, a wide smile spread across her lips.

"Oh, nothing." She chuckled, displacing the belt from her lap so she could stand. She tapped a finger against the wireframes. "With these, you truly do match my vision of a 'census taker.'"

He smiled, but it was small, and maybe a little pained, and she regretted the joke. It sounded similar to her harsh words when he'd first arrived. She chewed her lip, before adding, "But it's still you."

Eirlin slipped the glasses up to rest on top of his head. He blinked at her, startled, and she became keenly aware of how closely they stood. She took a step back, forcing a smile to hide the blush creeping up her cheeks.

"So, you're leaving?" she asked. It was a good distraction from whatever it was she had just done.

"Yes." He nodded. "I leave tomorrow."

"Oh," she murmured. She had anticipated the news, but still, the words brought a pang of sadness. "I'll miss you."

He looked startled again, and her lips twisted into a wry smile.

"What?" she asked, self-conscious of his shock. "I thought we were starting to become friends."

"No, no, you're right." He went to push his glasses up, but finding them missing, he moved his hand up to his head. His fingers bumped against his glasses and they slipped from their perch. Eirlin jerked forward, hands colliding with his as they both tried to catch the glasses.

"I'm sorry!" Eirlin kneeled to grab the wire rims. Carefully, she wiped snow from the glass. "They're fine."

She scrambled back to her feet, presenting the intact glasses.

"Thank you." Leiv smiled as he took them back, but for a moment, he simply looked at them in his hand. With a deep breath in, he slipped them back into place, then looked up at her again.

"I leave tomorrow," he began, words sudden and fervent. "But, with the information I've collected, I'll show the capital the merit of such data. And…"

Her head tilted at his pause. It was poignant, filling the slim space between them with that air of uncertainty she had come to expect between them ever since they had danced together.

She was finding it was a good kind of uncertainty.

"And," he finally continued, the fervency shifting into cautious constraint. "I will convince them to send me again. Next year."

"Next year," she repeated.

"Yes." He tapped the bridge of his glasses, then sighed and dropped his hand. "I must do what I can to protect our people, but I don't want to *forget* my people in the process."

"Next year," Eirlin said again, but this time without disappointment. "I look forward to that."

They came into that silence again, but this time, Leiv moved as if prepared for the pause he knew would come, with all its possibilities.

"I have something for you." He slipped a small pouch from his coat pocket and offered it to her. "As a thank you."

"A thank you?" Eirlin took the bag but kept Leiv pinned

with one perked eyebrow. "For what?"

"For helping me remember what's important."

The sarcastic eyebrow fell into scrunched confusion, and she stared at him hard, before looking down at the soft deerskin pouch in her palm. Gently, she tugged open the drawstring and peeked inside.

"Merkia helped me dye them," he began, when she simply stared down at the beads. They were beautiful, colors sharp and vibrant. "I hope they're what you need. For the red, I did try that new dyeing method, but I don't think—"

Eirlin engulfed him in a hug. At first, he stood stiffly beneath her, then, ever so slowly, he melted like a glacier on a summer day. His arms pulled up tight around her, nose digging into her hair, and she tightened her grip until she was certain her leather belt dug into them both.

Neither complained.

Build us up. At that moment, she was certain she had. The future was still uncertain, the past a fond memory, but Eirlin was content knowing that regardless of what would come, they would both fight for a future they could be proud of.

The bone beads were an assurance of more to come.

EPILOGUE

Neta

"I heard Leiv left," Neta said, dropping the length of rope beside Eirlin. Her mother had requested she wind it, and Neta obliged, though secretly wondering where she had obtained such a long length of cord.

She had expected Eirlin to say something, but all she got was a little huff of breath she assumed was an affirmative. Neta glanced down to where her friend sat, Esala's belt across her lap. The belt had become inseparable from Eirlin in the last few days; Neta was more shocked when she wasn't working on the thing.

"Nothing more to say, candidate?"

When even that title didn't rouse further words, Neta

lowered herself beside her friend and scrutinized her. Eirlin simply stared down at a small red bead held between her fingers.

"What's that?" Neta asked.

"A bead."

"Obviously." Neta rolled her eyes. "I've never seen one quite so red."

"Leiv dyed it."

"Oh?" A sly smile crept across Neta's face, and she glanced sideways at her friend. Eirlin was so easy to read. "That was kind of him."

"It was," she murmured, with the faintest of smiles.

"Did you kiss him?"

"What!" Eirlin gasped and finally tore her gaze away from the bead to stare agape at Neta.

"What?" Neta repeated slowly, wondering if she *had* misinterpreted her friend's furtive glances and nervous fidgeting. But then she saw the red running hot across Eirlin's cheeks, and she chuckled. "Oh, don't act so shocked. You'll get there."

About the Author

Lydia MacClaren has been writing stories since her earliest memories. *Bone Beads* is her first novella. She lives in rural Pennsylvania with her loving husband and sweet daughter. When she is not chasing around her toddler, she writes. When she is not writing, she dreams about her fictional worlds.

For more information about her future novels, including *The Bound*, visit www.lydiamacclaren.com.

If you enjoyed this story, consider leaving a review!